FIC
BROWN

VELVET

A Promised Land
Romance

VELVET

•

Carolyn Brown

AVALON BOOKS
NEW YORK

PRINTED IN THE UNITED STATES OF AMERICA
ON ACID-FREE PAPER
BY HADDON CRAFTSMEN, BLOOMSBURG, PENNSYLVANIA

To my friend, Andrea Shannon Hudgens.
Bless you for the past forty plus years.

Chapter One

Velvet Jane Dulan's soul left her body every time the wagon wheels hit a rut, but it didn't matter anymore. She was dying and she'd long since accepted the fact. The fever cracked her lips and wreaked havoc with her memory. She frowned, trying to recollect her sisters' faces before the fever took her off into a scary gray fog of nothingness. She'd die soon but she wanted to envision her four sisters one more time before she breathed her last.

She remembered telling them good-bye, all of them except Willow. She'd told her good-bye several weeks ago when she and Rafe Pierce finally realized they were made for each other. Willow looked so pretty even in her overalls and flannel shirt as she and Rafe rode off together after the wedding reception was over. Now that was truly something Velvet never expected to think. When she joined the wagon train and first saw Willow in men's clothing, she was mortified. But when Willow rode off that day, it seemed right as rain that she wore overalls and a flannel shirt.

She hung on to that idea for a while, then her mind shifted to another memory. The sisters were all sitting

1

around their little campfire one night and talking about something the stagecoach driver had told Willow when she reached St. Jo, Missouri. He'd said the hotel was full of fools waiting to go to California in their wagon trains; that they were all looking for the promised land, but there was no such place. Well, Willow had sure proven him wrong. She'd found her promised land and Velvet was happy for her youngest sister. Velvet would be seeing the real promised land before long and she had so wanted to stay around on Earth a little longer, so she could get to know her sisters better. After all, they'd only had a few weeks together.

Good-byes were important, she told herself as she drifted in and out of reality. They brought finality. Velvet didn't want to die but her body grew tired of fighting the fever for what seemed like forever. She wrinkled her brow and tightened her eyes, trying desperately to think about when the first symptoms had arrived. Heavy dark lashes lay on her hollowed cheek bones. A long, dark brown braid trailed down one side of her body, across a white lawn nightrail and three thick quilts she'd thrown off the upper part of her body when the fever reached temperatures so high it almost set her on fire. Her tormented brain couldn't remember when she hadn't been sick. All it could think about was the salty tears in Gypsy's eyes as she bent low and kissed Velvet's forehead; they felt like ice water on Velvet's fiery hot forehead. The aggravation in Garnet's face when she realized Velvet had to have medical help; and the worry etched in Gussie's forehead as she said good-bye. Velvet knew when she saw the womens' expressions that it wasn't just good-bye for a spell.

It was final. She was going to die.

Patty O'Leary saw the first Indian's teepees when the sun was still a big orange ball on the western horizon. "Faith and hallelujah," he muttered in his thick, Irish brogue. "If you are still breathin' lassy, rest assured that one of the O'Learys almost has you to a doctor. He'll make you well or this Irishman will come back and tack his sorry hide to the smokehouse door."

Velvet heard something about a smokehouse, but it was a muddle. They didn't have a smokehouse. She and her sisters had joined the train of mail-order brides more than two months ago. She tried to keep her eyes open a while longer, knowing that when they closed they'd never open again, but it was in vain.

"I need a doctor," Patty stretched his short frame as tall as he could in the wagon seat when the delegation of Indians rode out to meet him.

"What kind of sickness?" One brave peered over the back of the wagon.

"Don't know. Just high fever," Patty said, watching the braves turn heel and ride away as quickly as they could. Before he could reach the front gates of Fort Laramie, the Indians, who'd been camping outside the fort, were already tearing down their teepees and making ready to leave.

A uniformed sentinel waited at the gates. "State your business, sir," he said with more authority than his young face allowed, according to Patty O'Leary.

"I've got a sick woman who needs medical help," he said.

"We don't have a doctor no more," the man said. "All we have is a couple of stewards and a small clinic."

"No hospital?" Patty asked. Velvet Jane Dulan wouldn't live for sure if he had to haul her back those six miles to the wagon train. He didn't want to face the rest of those Dulan girls if he brought Velvet home dead.

"Haven't got it built yet. We did have a doctor, but he quit. Lives about two miles north of here if you want to take her there. He's gotten strange though since he quit practicing medicine. Had a lot of family problems and won't doctor no more," the man said.

"Well, he'll doctor this lass or he'll suffer the wrath of this Irishman. Two miles straight north?" Patty asked, narrowing his eyes and looking off in that direction.

"Just under, actually. Follow that trail right there. You'll come to a fork in the road. Stay right and keep going. Leads right up to Dr. Hoyt Baxter's cabin. He's a weird bird though. Might run you off with a shot gun. Tried to get him to look at a soldier that'd been wounded and he sent us packing. Cabin is right nice. You can't miss it, but I won't guarantee nothing," the man said. "What's the matter with her?"

"Fever of some kind," Patty said, but he didn't tell the man that they'd lost one woman on the wagon train with the same thing. They buried her yesterday and Hank was holding his breath that none of the others caught whatever it was that Velvet and the other woman had.

"Well, I couldn't let you pass through the gates with some unknown disease, anyway," the sentinel said. "Could be contagious and wipe us out."

"I see," Patty turned the wagon. Two miles. Well that was better than six back to the wagon train. That doctor would see her. Didn't matter what his past problems were, he wouldn't want to add the fury of the O'Leary clan to them. No sir, Dr. Hoyt Baxter was about to have a patient and that was not even the slightest bit of blarney.

"Hang on deary. We're about to go a little faster," he said over his shoulder, slapping the reins against the flanks of the two horses pulling the open wagon.

The cabin truly was a pretty little thing, with bright yellow flowers growing all around the porch, but nary a hound dog came out to meet him, so Patty O'Leary judged it a loveless home. Surely no one in their right mind would build a beautiful home and plant flowers, yet not have a good old friendly hound dog. Dr. Hoyt Baxter might not even get to smell the polish on the pearly gates if he was that stupid.

The short Irishman hopped off the wagon seat and wiggled some of the kinks from his back. Dust flew when he slapped his hat against the legs of his trousers. His boot heels made a rat-a-tat noise as he marched across the wooden porch. His patient was still breathing; shallowly, but breathing. He'd deliver her into the doctor's hands and at least be able to tell those spit-fire sisters of hers that she was alive when he left her. He knocked heavily upon the door but no one answered. He raised his fist and beat upon the door even harder, yelling out for the doctor as he did.

Still no answer.

"Faith and blasted luck," he mumbled as he tried the door. It was open so he marched into the living room as if it were his own home. A nice little front room with one of those winding staircases leading up to the loft, and a door just ahead that showed a neatly made bed. Well, Patty O'Leary might carry Velvet Jane Dulan into that bedroom but there wasn't anyway he could manage all that dead weight up those stairs. Besides the doctor was bound to come home sometime soon but it could be a while before he went up there. If Velvet was lying in his own bed, why, he'd be sure to find her.

Velvet didn't even flutter an eyelash when Patty threw the quilts off her body and picked her up. She had no idea when he laid her on the soft feather mattress or was aware of him tucking the quilts from the back of the wagon around her tightly.

"Now, something to write on," he said, looking around the room for a pencil or a scrap of paper. He found both in a small writing desk beside the fireplace. Good paper, too. Not the brown kind his sister used to make up her list for when she got into town. The tip of his tongue appeared at the corner of his mouth and he began to write the letter.

Dere doc. This here is Fel . . .

He scribbled out the words. Her name was Velvet and they'd all called her that, but her whole name was Velvet Jane. Patty didn't know how to spell Velvet. Now Jane was a different thing. His dear sister's name was Jane so he knew just how to make those letters. He smiled as he took up the pencil again.

Dere doc. This is Jane. She is sik. Help her. Thank U.

He stuck the note on a nail sticking out from one of the porch posts, unloaded her trunk onto the porch and drove away with a lighter heart. If that doctor didn't save her life, then her death would be on his hands. At least she hadn't died in Patty O'Leary's keeping. He checked the sky. He'd be back at the wagon train by bedtime. He hoped Annie had saved him some supper. She usually fed him and Hank at the end of the day, and Patty's mouth watered as he thought about one of her venison roasts.

Velvet knew she was alone in a strange place as she flitted around the edges of consciousness. Her trembling hands fumbled with the covers but the fever had long since drained her of all her strength. The misty, smoky fog lifted and she saw something akin to a light in the distance. Her fingers stopped the frantic fumbling and she was still, her countenance peaceful for the first time in more than a week.

Hoyt Baxter didn't understand the restlessness in his heart. He thought he'd finally gotten to the point in his life where everything was numb. Not peacefully numb; purely routine—nothing numb. No ups. No downs. Just nothing. Get up in the morning. Realize he was alone by his own making. Muddle through the day by doing chore upon chore. Go to bed at night and hope the dreams didn't come back to haunt him. Rise up with the sun and settle into the same rut again.

But that evening something inside Hoyt struggled. He wanted to sit on the porch and watch the sunset so he'd be finished with another day. One each day and then sometime in the future, he'd finally get to be an old man. Then he could do what he wanted to do so desperately—die! But a strange stirring mounted in his heart and restlessness overcame his miserable yet comfortable rut. Maybe he could walk it off, he thought as he paced from one end of the porch to the other. His uncut, thick dark hair lay on his shoulders and whipped across his strong, angular jaw every time he turned sharply and stomped across the wooden porch again. Dark brown eyes brooded with unbidden, unwanted memories: across the yard a vision of Myra playing with Bummer when he was a puppy; Boyd, riding up at breakneck speed on his big, black horse, to tell him they had need for him at the clinic; a happy, content Hoyt, leaning on the porch railing watching his beautiful wife, his twin brother, and the evening sun polishing off a perfect day.

Hoyt cleared the memories from his mind with a fierce shake of the head. The perfect days were gone. Just like all the good things in his life. He wouldn't think about them today. He'd take a long walk to tire him completely, then he'd come home and fall into a deep sleep where there were no yesterdays or horrid past mistakes to tear at his soul.

Bummer whined and cold-nosed his hand as he followed his master into the back yard and across the fields. Hoyt didn't stop and pet the big, black dog or even acknowledge his presence, but Bummer kept pace with the long strides his master took. Hoyt wondered if he kept walking and never looked back at the cabin, the barn, the corral, even the three tombstones under the shade tree out on the rise just north of the house, if the pain would diminish. No, because the pain wasn't in the house or any of the buildings. It wasn't even in the tiny cemetery that he kept spotlessly weed free. It was deep inside him and nothing would ever erase it.

He stopped at the back of his property and sat down on a grassy knoll. Bummer's ears perked up and he stared back toward the house. He whined and ran in that direction, looked back over his shoulder as if asking Hoyt why wasn't he following.

"Come back here, boy," Hoyt said, motioning with a flick of his wrist. The dog came back and sat obediently beside him. "She's not there, and she's not coming back," Hoyt said flatly. "Sit still and we'll go back in a few minutes." He finally rubbed the dog's ears absentmindedly.

Man and dog arose after more than half an hour. They stopped by the cemetery where Hoyt touched each of the tombstones. Tears flowed down his unshaven bristly cheeks and dripped on the stained collar of what used to be a snow-white shirt. Nowadays it was dull gray with stains. Myra would have been mortified to see him dressed like that, but Myra was gone so what did he care?

Bummer barked and every hair on his back stood straight up. Hoyt dried his eyes with the back of his hand and looked toward the house. A cloud of dust said a wagon was going back toward the fort. Probably a new steward at the clinic who didn't know Hoyt Baxter wasn't a doctor any more. At least not on anything but paper. He'd given up the rights to that title a year ago and he wasn't ever taking it up again.

Well, good riddance to an ignorant green horn. The only thing that amazed Hoyt was that the general hadn't told the steward not to bother coming out there. It didn't matter what the emergency was. The angels could leave Heaven and build snowmen on the north forty of Hell's acres before he used his medical knowledge again.

Bummer took off like a shot, barking and running toward the house. By the time Hoyt arrived, the dog was circling a big, roll-top steamer trunk on the porch. His growls would have put fear into any mortal being but they weren't doing a thing to remove the trunk. Hoyt's curiosity overrode the sorrow in his heart as he opened the trunk to find nothing but lady's clothing and a parcel of letters addressed to Miss Dulan. He didn't know anyone by the name of Dulan. Someone had delivered it to his house by mistake. She was most likely one of the new wives joining her soldier husband at the fort and her luggage had been sent to the wrong house. That was easily enough solved. Tomorrow he would load it on his wagon and carry it to the front gates where he'd unload it and drive away. He wouldn't go inside the fort. It was a solemn vow he'd made when he walked out of there a year ago, and he had no intentions of breaking it.

A soft breeze ruffled the letters. He shut the lid and started inside the house when he noticed the note on the porch post, flapping like it wanted to go back with the man who left it there.

"No!" Hoyt yelled when he'd read it. With it in his hand, he stormed through the front door like a bull. One look into the bedroom confirmed his fears. Some fool idiot who couldn't even spell had left a sick woman in his bed. Well, he wasn't going in there, much less taking care of her. How dare anyone just leave a sick woman in his house. He sat down at the kitchen table and put his head in his hands.

"She can breathe her last and I'll take her body and the trunk to the fort tomorrow morning," he declared.

Fifteen minutes later he edged toward the door. Her breathing was shallow; her skin, pale. Deep brown hair and dark lashes. A pretty woman probably in her healthy days; not so bad looking even so near death. And that's what she was courting because Dr. Hoyt Baxter could hear the rattling call from eternity in her throat.

"I will not," he declared and walked back out on the front porch. He opened the chest again and picked up the letters. He turned the top one over several times before he finally opened it, feeling guilty the whole time, yet he needed to know just who was dying in his house. The top letter was from her sister, someone named Gussie, who said that as soon as she was well, she should join up with the next wagon train and come on to Bryte, California. Husbands might all be taken but she could live with Gussie.

"Good grief," Hoyt put the letter back in the envelope. The woman had come from that foolhardy wagon train Hank Gibson was taking to the gold miners in California. A hundred women going to marry a hundred men. Mail-order brides. He'd heard about the wagon train. Even if that fool woman did live, she'd have a hard time finding anyone to take her to California because soon there wouldn't be any more trains until next spring. Besides, if she lived, it would be a month at least before she'd be ready to travel anywhere, and no train would be going to California that late in the year.

He went back inside the house and stared at her a while longer. Her breathing was even more shallow. Yes, she'd definitely be gone by morning, then his world could go back to its painful rut. "Of all the blasted luck," he finally mumbled and grabbed his black bag. He couldn't let her simply lay there and die. She might, no matter what he did, because his touch died a year ago, but he'd at least give it a try.

"Okay, Jane Dulan." He threw the patchwork quilts on the floor and picked up her wrist to take a pulse. "It's up to you, honey. If you live it'll be in spite of what I do, because everything I touch dies."

One moment she was traveling toward the beautiful,

beckoning light; the next, she was jerked back into a world of pain with someone literally prying her mouth open and pouring the most vile thing she'd ever tasted down her throat. She shivered and shook until she thought she'd lose her toenails, but she didn't open her eyes. She didn't want to look at the wicked devil making her swallow that dose.

Chapter Two

"Okay, Jane, open your mouth. If you don't eat, you don't live. And you are most definitely in a live or die situation here, Jane. You can live and get out of my house or your can die and get out of it. Frankly, I could care less," Hoyt said, his deep voice carrying through the void and into her subconscious.

Why did he keep calling her Jane? And who was he? Only Grandmother Tempton called her Jane, saying that Velvet was much too fancy a name for a child. Why, it could make a little girl vain to have a name like that and besides grown-up white women didn't name their children Velvet. Grandmother didn't know what her foolish daughter was thinking the day she and Jake Dulan named their one and only child. Now, Jane, that was a different matter. Grandmother said the name was plain and solid enough for any child to grow up with. Whoever kept putting chicken broth in her mouth must have known Grandmother, but it sure wasn't her high pitched whining voice Velvet heard. The voice was deep and resonant, and very masculine.

She opened her mouth but it was too much trouble to force her eyelids open. Blessed sleep was what she craved;

12

not weak chicken broth. What was it he said about a live or die situation? She tried to remember but it wouldn't come back to mind as she drifted off again.

The fever had been gone for two days. At first Hoyt had to put a spoon of medicine or broth in her mouth and then massage her throat gently to get her to swallow, but today she'd actually opened her mouth like a little bird and swallowed on her own. Progress, even if it was in small doses, was balm to a doctor's heart. Tomorrow she might open her eyes, but it would a couple of weeks before she would be on her feet again. At least a month before he could haul her and that trunk to the fort and be rid of the nuisance of having someone else in his home.

"Okay, Jane, I'm leaving now. You just keep on sleeping. It's the body's way of taking care of the damage that's been done to it," Hoyt said. He sponged off her face and neck with a wet wash cloth. She had been beautiful at one time and would be again. If it was a husband she yearned for, she could probably have her pick at the fort. There were two hundred and fifty unattached men there. Only about twelve had been brave enough to bring their wives out to this wilderness. He'd been one of those twelve, and for a while it was good. Now there were only eleven married women at the fort.

He broke half a dozen eggs into a crock bowl and whipped them up with a fork while two chicken legs sizzled in the grease. He would have preferred them rolled in flour and fried, but he had to boil them to make broth for Jane. He wouldn't think of her as his patient because she wasn't. She was just a woman he found in his bed three days ago, and he was nursing her back to health so she could go away. He tried to forget about her altogether as he watched a brown shell form on the chicken. Twice cooked. That's what Myra called it when she boiled a chicken then fried

the already cooked pieces. Most of the time she put a
healthy dose of black pepper on the boiled pieces and then
baked them, though. He wouldn't think about Myra. Not
today. He wouldn't think about her or Boyd or Weston.
He'd think about making his breakfast and whether or not
Jane was ready to eat real food yet. Maybe, he would dice
one of the breasts and see if he could talk her into chewing
later today. Then he would cut the other one up into some
dumplings for himself.

He checked his cattle after breakfast. One brown and
white Hereford had produced a healthy bull calf during the
night. He'd keep both of them, but come fall, he'd cull out
the herd, selling off those he didn't want to winter to one
of the drives going on north into Montana. He came back
to the cabin at noon and Jane chewed two bites of chicken
before she refused to open her mouth anymore. Hoyt took
that as a good sign and he and Bummer worked all afternoon cleaning out the hay loft in the barn, getting it ready
to store the new crop.

At supper she managed a few more bites of chicken. He
wondered when she'd finally wake up and realize she
wasn't on a wagon train any more. Not that it mattered. He
kept telling himself he'd do the same for old Bummer if
he was lying half dead on the porch. Truth was, he could
hardly wait for her to wake up and get better if she was
going to do so. Didn't seem right, her lying in Myra's bed
like that. Her head on Myra's pillow and besides all of
which he wasn't sleeping worth a hoot up there in the loft.
He liked his own bed even if it was terribly lonely when
he awoke in the middle of the night and reached for Myra,
only to find she wasn't there.

He propped his feet on the porch rail and watched dusk
fall. When it was fully dark, he rubbed Bummer behind the
ears and went inside to climb the stairs to the loft. He
bumped his head on the rafters while he was taking off his

shoes. "Blasted loft wasn't intended for a six-foot-man," he muttered. He sat down on the bed to remove his suspenders and trousers, only to hit his shoulder on the bed post. Yes, Hoyt Baxter would be elated to have his room back and sleep in his own bed.

When Velvet Jane first opened her eyes, she lay very still for a long time. It was so peaceful with the moon dawning in the window, the sound of crickets chirping somewhere in the house, a frog lamenting outside the window and a dog growling at something in the distance. The glow of the white moon filled the bedroom window, giving a strange light to the objects in the room. Was this Heaven? Was Heaven really nothing more than a continuation of life only on a different plane?

She tried to lift her hand but it took too much effort. Sitting up would be completely out of the question. She flicked her tongue out to moisten her dry, cracked lips. Fever. She'd had a high, hot fever and they thought she was going to die so they'd sent her to the doctor at Fort Laramie. That must be where she was, but this didn't look like any hospital room she'd ever seen in South Carolina. Her aqua blue eyes darted around the room, taking in everything in a glance, then going back for details. It was a woman's bedroom. Maybe even a couple's bedroom from what she could discern. Lace curtains blowing gently with the breeze coming in the window said a woman lived here. But a man's presence permeated the room as surely as if he was sitting in the big oversized rocking chair in the corner.

Turning her head to look out the window took most of her energy, but the moon captivated her attention. She hadn't died. The moon proved it. She was alive and she couldn't even sit up in this strange place. Just exactly where had Patty O'Leary taken her? She wondered. But not for long, because no matter how hard she tried, she couldn't stay awake long enough to find out.

When she awoke again it was to the smell of something frying, and a man mumbling to himself on the other side of the door. She licked her lips and hoped that his wife, whoever she was, would bring something to her, soon. Her stomach set up a rumble as if to say now that she was going to live, she needed sustenance. Even in the coolness of the early morning, the quilts on top of her were heavy weights. She raised a hand to push them away but didn't have the strength to fight with even one, much less all three of the hefty patchwork quilts.

Hoyt slathered a pancake with butter and topped it off with maple syrup. He'd eaten his fill and figured if Jane could chew bits of chopped chicken, she should be able to eat soft pancakes. He threw open the door to find her eyes wide open and her hands fumbling with the covers. Her eyes were the strangest color he'd ever seen. Big round eyes filled with sky blue water, yet there was a little green thrown in with dark lashes outlining them. Beautiful eyes, but deadly, because if he was reading them right, and looks could kill, he'd be dead before he could hit the wooden floor.

"Well, you are awake," he said gruffly. "That's good because if you're going to live I'm taking you to the fort. They can take care of you there."

"Who are you?" She formed the words slowly and they came out in a raspy whisper.

"I'm Hoyt Baxter and let's set this straight from the beginning. I don't appreciate whoever left you in my bed. Matter of fact, if I could get my hands on that fool he'd be visiting with St. Peter by nightfall. I don't want you here and the quicker you can get out the better I'll like it," he said.

"Where am I?" she asked just as laboriously.

"Couple of miles from Fort Laramie and you've been here three days. Your wagon train is probably long since gone, so you'll have to make some other arrangements to go find your mail-order husband. For right now, though, you are going to have some food. Get your strength back. And then you can get out of my house, Jane Dulan." Hoyt sat down in the straight-backed chair beside the bed, covered her neck and chest with a cloth napkin and cut off a small bite of pancake.

"Velvet," she said.

"Nope, pancakes. Might feel like velvet when you get them in your mouth, but they're just pancakes," he said.

"My name is Velvet," she said, her eyes shooting daggers into his handsome face.

"Velvet is not a name. It's a material women use to make fancy ball dresses. You are not a Velvet. You are a Jane. The note on my porch said your name was Jane and that's what you are. Just a plain old Jane. Now open your mouth."

She clamped it shut and shook her head as much as her weak neck muscles would allow. Hoyt Baxter might be the most handsome man she'd ever set her eyes upon, and he might have in his possession the most delicious pancakes in the whole world, but he wasn't going to treat her like a child. She'd come through the valley of the shadow of death and she lived. And by golly, there wasn't a man alive who was going to tell her what name she was using. Not when she'd decided to be Velvet when she left South Carolina and traveled all the way to St. Jo, Missouri to see her father. She would be Velvet or she'd starve. This Hoyt Baxter, whoever the devil that was anyway, could accept it or get out of the way and she'd force herself out of the bed and make her own breakfast.

"I said open your mouth, Jane," he demanded, his brown eyes flashing and the muscles of his square, masculine jaws working in anger.

"Velvet," she said through clenched teeth.

Blasted woman, he thought, his eyes drawn into mere slits. "I don't care if your name is Cow Patty or Queen Victoria. Just open your mouth and eat something so I can get about my business. A ranch doesn't run itself, not even in the summer time in Wyoming."

"Velvet," she said, her voice stronger this time.

"Okay, okay, you win. If you're going to sleep in my bed while you get well, then Velvet it is. I don't like that name. Jane fits you better and it's a decent name. Velvet sounds like something a person would name a slave child," Hoyt said, glad though that she opened her mouth.

A slave child, she thought. *Well, what better name then. Even if my skin isn't the right color or my eyes either, that's pretty much what I've been my whole life. My grandparents owned me, or thought they did. Too bad they didn't have papers saying I was their slave or they could've kept me in South Carolina and really forced me to marry that old man.*

She forgot about his caustic manner as she held the first bite of the pancake in her mouth a while before chewing it. Nothing had ever tasted better than that pancake, and she ate every single bite of it. "More," she said, "and coffee, too?"

"Well, Vel—l—l—vet!" He drew the name out in true southern fashion, his very tone poking fun. "I do believe you have survived the fever. With an appetite like this you should be out of my house in a couple of weeks."

"Days, Mr. Baxter," she said just as sarcastically.

"That would be a miracle," he snapped. "There's more pancakes on the stove warmer. I'll bring another one and a cup of coffee, too. Cream and lots of sugar?"

"Black. Strong and hot," she said, her eyes battling his. Whoever he was, he sure had a burr in his saddle concerning women. The soft southern accent in his voice said he was from the south where gentlemen honored their women folks. Did he come from a family who had slaves? Maybe one of them was named Velvet and he didn't like that person. She wove stories in her mind as she waited for the rest of her breakfast.

So she liked her coffee strong, black and hot, well Hoyt Baxter could deliver that. Just exactly what kind of woman was she anyway? He expected her to whimper in fear when she awoke and found a man bringing her breakfast. The least she could do was thank him for saving her sorry life, but no, she had to fight with him the first rattle out of the bucket over something as stupid as her name. Velvet *was* a slave's name, too. He hadn't been telling tall tales. His uncle, Henry Baxter, kept slaves in Georgia and the cook's name was Velvet. She made the best blackberry cobbler in the whole state of Georgia. Hoyt remembered asking his mother as they traveled back to Louisiana if they could steal Velvet and take her home.

You got your Velvet now, his conscience teased. *She's white and she's got the bluest eyes in the state of Wyoming, and she probably don't know squat about making a pie, but you got a Velvet in there. Twenty years after the day you and Boyd were eight and you asked for her, but you got her. Wonder what Boyd would think of her?*

"Don't matter what Boyd would think," he muttered in a hateful tone. "Myra would hate the whole thing."

Velvet was struggling to sit up when he marched through the door, his boots sounding like cannon fire with every step. When she got to Bryte, California, she intended to give Patty O'Leary a sizable chunk of her mind for leaving her at the mercy of some rancher named Hoyt Baxter. He could have taken her to the fort where there was a proper hospital and doctors.

"Little weak are you, in spite of your sassy tongue?"

Hoyt set the plate on the dresser and slipped his strong arms around her, lifting her into a sitting position as easily as if she'd been nothing more than a weak kitten.

"Yes," she said. "But I will get stronger." Stronger so that a man's arms touching her didn't make shivers shoot up her backbone. Stronger so she could hitch a ride on the next wagon train and go on to join her sisters. Stronger so she could do just what Hoyt Baxter wanted . . . get out of his house and his life.

"Let's hope so," he said. "And soon." He picked up the cup of coffee. "The coffee is hot so sip it," he said, holding it up to her lips.

Not even the delicious pancakes or maple syrup could compare with that first taste of coffee. The bitter warmth journeyed slowly all the way to her stomach and revitalized her. It might be days before she was ready to walk however many miles it was to Fort Laramie, but that first sip of coffee reminded her that Velvet Jane Dulan was not dead; she was alive, albeit a sticky, dirty mess of a woman who needed a bath.

Alternately she had bites of pancake and sips of coffee until they were both gone. Hoyt could scarcely believe that a woman who'd actually kissed death on the cheek could eat like that. He'd expected her to nibble around the edges of breakfast and then go back to sleep. In all of his doctoring, he had never even seen a soldier come out of a fever-induced coma that hungry. Most southern women—he'd eat his boots and have his spurs for dessert, if Velvet Jane Dulan wasn't from the deep south—would have been embarrassed to put away that much food in front of a man. They might eat like field hands when no one was looking, but they were trained from childhood to be simpering, dependent women. *At least out in public,* he thought. *Mother is one of the strongest women I know, but then she isn't the normal southern woman.*

"Need a bath," she said.

"I suppose I could do that, too. After all, I don't have a ranch to run or cows to take care of. I just sit in that there rocking chair and wait to see what my almost dead patient wants me to do," he said gruffly.

The blush started at her toes and warmed her skin all the way to the roots of her hair. "You will not," she said, inching her way back down into the bed. She might be weak but she would fight him; tooth, hair, fingernails and eyeballs if he so much as even tried to take her nightrail off. When she saw Patty O'Leary again, she just might do more than give him a lecture. She might shoot him graveyard dead.

"And I suppose you'll do it yourself. You can't even lift yourself up into a sitting position," he said. "Don't worry Lady Velvet. I'm a doctor. No, I'm not. I used to be a doctor. I could bathe you and never even notice that you were different from the soldiers on the base."

"No!" She said, the one word hanging heavy between them. She'd never felt so dirty in her whole life—or so belittled. "Put a tub of water over there and I can do it. Later, today, when I'm stronger."

"Sure!" Hoyt laughed. "I'll put the tub right there. Three feet from the bed. Then I'm going on about my morning business. If you fall on the floor in a heap, that's where you'll stay all day. If you drown, then I'll cart your naked carcass to the fort and they can bury you in their cemetery. I didn't ask for you to be left in my bed, and I'm sure not going to waste any more time on you."

"Fine," she said, turning her head to look out the window. The dawning of the moon had been only a few hours ago when she'd first opened her eyes and realized that she wasn't going to die. What happened to the peace she'd felt when she saw that big white moon framed in the window? It had sure enough flown right out the same window when

Hoyt Baxter walked in the room. Velvet declared silently that she'd live, all right. If for no other reason than to show Hoyt Baxter that she could. It might take her all day long to talk her weak muscles into walking three feet and crawling into a tub of water, but she'd do that, too. And she'd be out of his house so fast he'd wonder in coming years if there ever was a woman left on his bed.

She'd do it all, because as soon as she could, she wanted out. She didn't care if it was on a wagon train going west to California or if she had to buy a horse to take her east back to Lewellen, Nebraska where her youngest sister Willow lived. Anywhere, as long as Hoyt Baxter wasn't there.

Chapter Three

Still propped up on pillows Velvet watched Hoyt bring in an oval tub from the back porch and park it no more than three feet from the end of the bed. The chair legs made a grating sound as he dragged a cane-bottomed ladder-back chair across the wood floor. She jumped when he dropped it with a loud thud. He opened a drawer in an oak bureau and took out a washcloth and snowy white bath towel, along with a cake of milled soap. The soft breeze floating through the room brought the sweet smell of lavender to Velvet's nose, but that's all that was sweet. Hoyt Baxter looked like he could kill someone, preferably someone named Velvet Jane Dulan. She'd never seen a man with so many sullen, black looks, and absolutely no humor in his dark eyes.

"Where's your wife?" She asked.

"That's none of your business. But she's gone and she won't be back," he answered, laying the bath supplies on the chair. "I'll fill this tub up and from then on it's up to you. I'm going about my work."

"What's her name?" Velvet asked.

"Nosy, aren't you? Her name's Myra, and that is the last

of the questions I'm answering," Hoyt told her. When he said Myra there was a softness in his voice and on his face. So he was a married man. His wife left him and would never return. He used to be a doctor, probably at Fort Laramie since he lived so close to it, she surmised as she watched him. On first opinion, she'd figured him for a heartless man, but there was a definite softness when he spoke his wife's name. Whatever had happened in the past had surely soured him on life, but he'd get through it some-day. And she'd be long gone when he did. She wasn't there to help some wandering soul find its way back home. She was there to get well, thanks to Patty O'Leary, who'd better keep his Irish mouth shut when she saw him again and his big old Irish ears open, because he was in for the dressing down of his life.

Velvet was weak as a kitten. Her reputation was thoroughly ruined because she'd spent several nights in the same house with a married man. She didn't care one bit about any of it. Not the information she'd gleaned concerning Hoyt, or her reputation. She just wanted a bath and getting it was going to take all the strength she could possibly muster.

He filled the tub without another word and then marched resolutely out of the house, slamming the front door so hard it rattled the glass windows in the front room. In addition to being a doctor, Hoyt Baxter was a fool with a temper. Glass windows weren't cheap and they didn't grow on scrub ash trees. If he would've broken one of the two window panes, he would have had to board up the hole. That made him a fool in Velvet's eyes. The temper probably came from which ever parent gave him all that thick gorgeous black hair and those brown eyes.

"He'd better not break my window," she said, looking out across the back yard toward the barn where Hoyt was saddling up a horse. "Because I intend to watch the dawning of the moon every night I'm in this place and he'll get a taste of Dulan temper if he breaks that window and has to board it up."

The first order of business was to push the quilts off her feeble frame and swing her legs over the side of the bed. That took twenty minutes and more energy than she ever imagined, but she was determined to wash the grime from her body. She was glad her jelly-filled legs weren't able to carry her to the mirror above the bureau. She didn't want to see what she looked like after more than a week of illness and dirt. Most likely her face was even a bigger smudged mess than her hands and fingernails. Maybe Hoyt Baxter thought she was a mixed breed runaway slave and deserved the name Velvet. If her face was as dirty as the rest of her body, she couldn't blame him one bit. Then she remembered him sponging her face with a damp cloth. Maybe it was at least somewhat clean.

She was sitting on the side of the bed, trying to sweet talk her feet and legs into supporting her when he came storming back in the front door, dragging something heavy across the floor. He swung open the bedroom door without knocking and left her trunk at the foot of the bed. Without a word, he turned and went back out, this time leaving the door wide open.

She'd made progress. Sitting up like that on the side of the bed took a great deal out of a person who'd laid for days with a fever. He'd seen six foot soldiers sweat bullets just trying to keep upright the first time they sat up. She had stamina, that Velvet Dulan did. He'd have to give her that much. But she sure couldn't crawl out of that bed and take a bath all alone. He'd find her laid out like a corpse when he got home, either eager to shed her modesty and let him help her with a bed bath, or else grasping her modesty like a cloak of righteousness, and willing to lay there in all that sticky, fever-induced, dried sweat for a few more days.

There is no hurry, she kept repeating to herself. She had all day and even if the water turned cold as ice, it would still feel good on her skin after more than a week of lying in bed, stewing in her own juices. She eased the bottom of her nightrail up around her waist, and had half a mind to lay back down for a few minutes. Not a long time, but maybe five minutes.

"No!" She said emphatically, knowing that if she fell back into those inviting feather pillows, she wouldn't rise up off of them. The bath could wait, but her rebellious pride couldn't. And Velvet didn't intend to lose one bit of her newly earned self-esteem. What would her spit-fire little sister Willow do in the same circumstance?

"She'd rise up, grab a cup of water and whip a forest fire," Velvet said with a smile, the first since she'd succumbed to the fever. She hadn't felt well in several days but managed to keep the sisters from knowing until she collapsed walking along beside the wagon. They put her to bed inside the covered wagon, and she remembered something about them loading her into the back of a wagon. Gussie, Garnet and Gypsy told her good-bye and Patty O'Leary hauled her away. The next thing she knew she opened her eyes to the beautiful dawning of the moon in the bedroom window.

That was last night and she'd eaten a good breakfast so maybe she could at least make it three feet to the bathtub. She tested her legs and they gave way, spilling her out onto the floor, a heap of bones and loose flesh tangled up in a dirty white nightrail. She lay there several minutes, deciding one moment that the lack of stamina was just like a forest fire and she didn't even have a cup to haul water to fight it, and the next chastising her own thoughts for having no gumption.

"You will get up," she said breathlessly, then eyed the tub of water then realized she didn't have to get up on her weak legs and walk to the tub. She merely had to crawl over there, wiggle out of the gown and use the last of her reserve to fall over the side into the water. Once inside, she didn't have to hurry. Velvet crawled, wiggled, fell and then finally sighed when the cool water splashed over her body.

Her arms trembled when she reached for the soap but she held it firmly. If she dropped it, she'd never retrieve it, and it had been months since she'd had a bath with real scented soap. It took more than an hour for her to lather her body and rinse the soap away.

"Swim or drown," she said with the last breath left in her tired body. Then she let go of the sides of the tub, drew her knees up and let her head fall back into the water. She'd either drown or she'd have clean hair when the ordeal was finished. Velvet figured clean hair was worth the chance. Dark brown hair, highlighted with chestnut streaks, floated out around her like a halo. Once it was wet, she forced her legs to push her body back into a sitting position and lathered her hair with the soap. She really thought maybe she would drown by the time she got all those bubbles out of her hair, but caught a second wind and finished the job in fine style.

"Now how do I dry myself sitting bare-hiney naked, dripping water on the floor?" She wondered aloud. "Or better yet, how do I open that trunk and dig around for clean clothing? What would Willow do?"

Willow would manage to find some way just to show Hoyt Baxter who was boss, that little voice deep inside her said. *Remember how she rode a horse right into the middle of that wagon train to thwart those dangerous men? Well, pretend you are Willow and do whatever you have to do.*

"No, I won't," she argued with herself. "I'll do it because I'm showing Hoyt who's boss, but I'm doing it because

I'm Velvet Dulan and I'm every bit as sassy and mean as any of my other four sisters. They said I'd find my streak when I needed it. Well, I need it now and I'll find it."

She managed to throw a leg over the edge of the cold tub and flop out, not totally unlike a bass flipping out of the river onto dry land. The water made circles on the wood floor where she lay flat on her back, staring at the rafters supporting the roof of the house. She pulled the bath sheet from the chair and covered herself with it until she could find the strength to sit upright. Hoping that Hoyt didn't find another reason to come barging in the house, she stripped off the sheet and dried her long, long hair. By the time her shaking arms finished that job, the rest of her body had air dried so she crawled to the trunk. Lifting the lid was no easy feat but she managed on the fourth or fifth try after opening it a few inches and then throwing all her weight into tossing it open. Her comb was in the small top tray, along with a packet of letters addressed to Miss Dulan. They hadn't been there the last time she opened the trunk, so evidently they were either from Hank or the sisters. She'd read them later when she was dressed.

With only the bath sheet draped over her, she meticulously combed every tangle from her hair and then braided it into two long ropes, one hanging down each side. Her stomach growled, still expecting to be fed three times a day. Old habits were hard to break, even in illness. Hoyt had said he wouldn't return until supper time and left no doubt he'd be tickled pink to find her drowned or dead. With that in mind, she figured the only way she'd have lunch was to figure out a way to get into that kitchen and scrounge around for leftovers. Maybe there was another pancake on the stove. Or better yet, if she could reach the can of maple syrup, maybe she'd just turn it upside down and drink it. At least it would ease her grumbling stomach.

She rested the better part of an hour after the strenuous

job of doing her hair and then very gently pulled herself up onto her knees to peer inside the trunk. They quivered and protested, but she stiffened the muscles as best she could and rummaged around until she had a pair of drawers and a camisole in her hands. If he found her dead at least she wouldn't be naked when he hauled her to the cemetery at Fort Laramie.

Another hour went by before she finally had the under clothing on, and had a calico dress laid across her lap. Tired to the bone, hungry enough to eat fried poke salad which she hated with a passion, yet proud of herself for her accomplishments, she raised the heavy dress over her head and let it fall.

"It doesn't weigh eighty pounds," she mumbled. "Only seems that way." She shoved her arms into the sleeves and fastened two buttons before she had to stop and catch her breath again. By the time she was fully dressed, she could have truly drunk two gallons of pure maple syrup, but she didn't have the foggiest notion of how to stand up and go to the kitchen without falling hind end over tea kettle back into the dirty bath water.

"Never waste water," she reminded herself in her grandmother's voice. She picked up her dirty nightrail and pitched it into the water. After she figured out a way to eat, she'd come back and do the laundry.

She crawled into the kitchen on her hands and knees, going a foot and resting five minutes. When she reached the cold cook stove, she used the handle on the oven door to hoist herself to her knees, and then up on her legs. Surprisingly, she didn't fall and even more miraculously, there was a stack of four pancakes left sitting there. She wobbled when she reached for them, but her legs held in spite of enough shaking to resemble a full-fledged earth quake.

Two steps and she plopped down ungracefully in a chair at the table, but she clutched the pancakes in her hand. She chewed them slowly, relishing each bite as if it were manna from Heaven. Let Hoyt Baxter come home now. Just let that obnoxious, egotistical, handsome man come home and find that she had a backbone. It might be aching and tired, but it was ramrod straight. She might not be able to get back into that room except on her hands and knees but she could do it, and by golly, she could do it on her own. She was a Dulan, and they were made of iron nerves and sass.

Hoyt rode out to the back side of his property and cut hay all day long. After a few days of drying, he'd haul it back to the barn. Winters were long and hard in Wyoming and he'd need lots of good hay when snow fell deep to keep his cows alive until the next spring when the new minty green grass finally peeped out from the cold earth.

He skipped lunch, ignored his rumbling stomach and argued with himself over the woman he'd left sitting on the side of the bed. Even with his medical knowledge he didn't have any idea what kind of fever she'd had, or why she'd finally shaken it off, but no doubt she'd had an up close and very personal visit with Death itself. She should have swung her legs over the edge of the bed and fainted like most blue-blooded women. And most big, healthy men, too, if the truth be told.

He could have stayed, used that old Baxter bedside manner and talked her into letting him, purely as a doctor, help her take a bath. But the Dr. Baxter bedside manner was gone . . . just like Myra. Just like Boyd. All gone.

He wondered if she'd truly figured out a way to get into that bath. She certainly needed one after sweating that much. He could smell her when he walked through the door to bring her breakfast that morning. Controlling the snarl on his nose had taken more than a little will power. Knowing that she couldn't help the condition, and not wanting to upset her when she found out that she'd been staying with a man with no woman in the house all that time, kept him from telling her just how bad she was making *his* bedroom stink. Then the wretch turned on him, demanding that she be called Velvet instead of Jane, and creating a stir in his emotions that he didn't want.

He'd vowed last year that he'd never doctor again or that nothing would ever make him feel again. Not anything. Not a woman. Not a patient. Nothing. He'd been raised to believe suicide was the most cowardly act in the world, so he had to go on living. But he didn't have to feel. Not pain. Not love. Not rage. Velvet had sure enough raised his anger factor to an all time high. For that, he slapped his hand against his thigh. It stung and he grimaced. Pain and pure old madness all in one day. She'd made him break his solemn vow and he hoped when he got home she was sprawled out on the floor graveyard dead.

No, he didn't. He wouldn't wish death upon anyone. She had sisters who he'd feel compelled to write to, and their hearts would be broken. He'd known that kind of torment and he didn't want that even for his worst enemy. He revised his wish, and hoped she'd fallen back on the pillows and was out cold again. That she wouldn't even open her eyes when he fed her a few bites of supper. And most of all that she would heal quickly and be gone soon out of his life so he could go on living in his lackluster world for the rest of his days.

He and Bummer stopped at the barn long enough to unsaddle the horse and rub him down. Hoyt had jumped two rabbits that afternoon in the hay field and shot both of them. They'd be good fried up in bacon grease with some onions. Maybe he'd even make gravy and biscuits to go with them. Velvet might like that.

A low growl erupted from his throat and he shook his head violently. What she liked or didn't like shouldn't even be a factor in what he made for his own supper. She could eat whatever he had and be glad to get it. Bummer remembered back when Hoyt growled like that when they were playing and nosed the back of his hand. Hoyt jumped four inches off the ground.

"You stupid dog," he grumbled. A smile twitched at the corners of his strong, sensuous mouth but it didn't materialize and it didn't reach his eyes. "She'd be laughing her head off if she saw you scare me. She thinks I'm the big bad boogie man, and I want her to keep thinking that," he confided in a whisper to the dog.

He threw open the front room door to find her dressed, her hair nicely braided, sitting up in bed, leaning back amongst the pillows, and the whole house smelling faintly of lavender. Her face was gaunt but her blue eyes were very much alive. The dress hung on her slight frame but it was buttoned all the way up the front.

"Well, why didn't you take this stinky water out and dump it?" He asked. "And why didn't you cook my supper? Man keeps you alive and you just lay here all day long."

"Why don't you ride a poker straight to the bowels of Hades and kiss the Devil right smack on the lips?" She said right back at him.

A chuckle came nigh onto gagging him, but he wouldn't let it out. He didn't want to fool Velvet one bit. His eyes might give him away. They actually twinkled and his mouth twitched as he kept the grin at bay.

"Right sassy aren't you?" He said as he dragged the tub through the kitchen and out the back door. While it emptied, he held his sides and rocked with silent laughter. He wouldn't let her know, not in a million years, how laughing until he had to wipe his eyes made him feel almost like a human being again.

"See you ate up the leftover pancakes," he grumbled when he went back inside, but it didn't sound near as menacing as it did earlier that day. "Now I guess old Bummer will have to go hungry."

"Who is Bummer?" She asked.

"My dog," he answered.

"No, he won't go hungry. You can cook something else. I saw those two rabbits you threw on the table, Hoyt Baxter. And I bet you can make a fine gravy to go with them," she said, her mouth already watering.

"And I bet you can eat a whole one by yourself," he said, lighting the kindling in the fire box.

"Two, most normally. But since I've been ailin', maybe one would do. You can share yours with Bummer," she said. Lord, if she got a rabbit leg down along with a bit of gravy on a biscuit, she'd be so full she'd probably gag. Her stomach almost rebelled at that last bite of fist-sized pancakes.

"Not on your life, Vel—l—l—vet," he said. "You can share yours."

She just smiled and shut her eyes.

He'd gotten the last word so why did he feel like he'd lost the whole blasted war?

Chapter Four

The next day when Hoyt went away, Velvet held onto the bed stead and other bits of furniture and walked to the door, once an hour all day long. She'd never felt so physically weak and she hated it. She was used to rising early and walking ten to fifteen miles a day with the wagon train. Now she was reduced to panting after ten to fifteen feet. She'd get well or she'd literally die trying. The following day, Hoyt brought her breakfast and disappeared back into the living room, but he didn't put his boots on.

Conversation had been almost nonexistent the past two days, but that was fine with Velvet. When she could walk out of this crazy cabin she fully intended to do just that.

Hoyt was glad she was closemouthed. He didn't want to listen to endless questions about his past. He didn't need a friend and he sure wasn't going to tell a complete stranger named, of all things, Velvet, his life story.

"Why aren't you going out to work?" Velvet asked when he took the empty plate from her hands.

"Because today is Sunday," he said.

"Oh, is it really? Are you going to church then at the Fort?"

See, he thought, *questions into my life.* "Yes, it is really and no I am not. I will read a while after I put a venison roast in the oven to eat today, and maybe sit on the porch with Bummer. Does that answer all the questions you've got?" He asked grumpily.

"You don't have to be hateful," she said. "When you're riding on a wagon train there are no Sundays. It's just another day, and since I lost track of days when I was ill, I had no idea it was Sunday."

He didn't answer. After he washed her plate and fork, dried them and set them on the shelf above the stove, he picked up his worn black Bible and sat down in the rocking chair, his back to the bedroom door. He liked Sundays in the winter best of all, when it was cold outside and the fireplace roared with fire and warmth. Today, there was at least a nice breeze blowing through the open front door. If there hadn't been a nosy woman taking up his space he wouldn't have even minded a summer Sunday to read his Bible.

Velvet threw her legs over the side of the bed and stood up. Using the bedpost for a handrail she went all the way to the door and slammed it shut. So what if it rattled the window panes. He didn't have to be so curt. It was her reputation on hot coals. People at the fort where she'd have to stay for a while wouldn't care if he had a woman on his place. Oh, no, the old double standard would stand firm and true. A man could do what he wanted and society winked at it. But, let a woman do the same thing and society crucified her. She threw open the trunk lid without a hitch and pulled her nightrail over her head. In ten minutes she was fully dressed but for shoes, and who needed them when there was no chance she'd get outside the cabin?

She picked up her Bible, stiffened her back and opened the door. Out of anger and determination, she walked across the living room floor to the other rocking chair and sat down gracefully. She let her Bible fall open and began to read the short book of James concerning what all faith could produce in the Christian life.

"Another week and you'll be strong enough to get out of here," he said, looking up from his readings in Job.

"I certainly hope so." She didn't take her eyes off the page, but she couldn't see a word for the blur. Whether it was fear of the unknown about what would happen to her at the fort, or just plain exasperation for the predicament she was in, she didn't know. She just wished she was back on the wagon train and walking her fifteen miles a day. If only she could wake up and this would all be some kind of crazy dream, she'd be as happy as a singing lark. She wouldn't even complain about having to marry someone she didn't know at the end of the journey. Especially if he had a better attitude than Mr. Hoyt Baxter.

He didn't look up for a solid hour, at which time he laid his Bible on the fireplace mantel, put on his shoes and walked out the door without so much as a grunt in her direction. She slowly walked back into the bedroom, put her own Bible in the trunk and stared again at the framed paper on the wall declaring that Captain Hoyt Baxter was a doctor. Too bad it didn't say anything about why he wasn't one any longer.

In a few minutes she found herself on the porch, eyeing a swing at one end. She sat down carefully and pushed off with a bare foot, enjoying the motion and the cool morning breeze. If all of Wyoming was as beautiful as this area, it's a wonder the wagon trains headed toward California ever got past Fort Laramie. The skies were more blue than anything she'd ever seen before and the foliage was a rich, deep green. Even the hills of South Carolina couldn't rival the panoramic sight before her that morning. She'd heard Patty O'Leary say the winters in this area were dreadful, but it was hard to believe anything in Wyoming could be that bad—except Hoyt Baxter.

"Speak of the devil," she mumbled when he rode past her. She wondered if he was going to the fort but a quick check of the sun's position let her know he was riding north and the fort was somewhere south of the ranch.

Hoyt had no intentions of altering his Sunday ritual. Velvet Dulan wasn't worth it, and besides, as fast as she was getting around, by next Sunday she'd be just a faint memory. He already had it in mind to take her to the fort no later than Friday or maybe he'd just send her back with Rooster, an old man who came to the fort once a month for supplies. Rooster was the one man who understood exactly why he'd quit the service and doctoring, too. Rooster brought supplies out to him about once every other month until winter hit and this was the week he should arrive. Yes, that's what he'd do; just send her along with Rooster. She had a healthy appetite and could walk from one room to the other now without holding on to the walls or the furniture. She must come from some sturdy stock to heal as fast as she did.

He didn't urge his horse to a trot but kept the pace slow just like he had done every Sunday for the last year. Sunday wasn't a day to hurry even if he did have a lot to discuss with them today. A small cemetery with a white picket fence surrounding it lay under a shade tree at the top of a rise. Hoyt slid off the horse's back and tethered the reins to the fence. He opened the gate, reminded himself to bring some oil next week to put on the squeak, and closed it gently behind him. He dropped down on his knees before the three graves and bowed his head.

"Well, you'll never believe what has happened this week. I came home from the fields one day and there's a woman layin' in the bedroom. I didn't want her to be there and I've been pretty tacky. I know, I know, it's not the Christian way to do things, but she'll be gone in a few days and I'll ask forgiveness for my black heart."

Bummer watched over the man, the horse and the graves like he did every Sunday. But today it was especially hard because he could feel the thunder of lots of horses coming from the north, and he wanted to run back to the cabin and protect it. He growled deep in his throat but the man didn't stop talking and didn't budge from his position.

Velvet heard the noise before she saw the horses bearing down on the ranch as if they intended to run right through the house. She stood up, leaned on the porch post and shaded her eyes. It resembled a stampede and for a moment she wondered if Hoyt had been caught up in the thing since that was the direction in which he'd ridden off. Then the mass took form and she realized it was horses, not cattle, coming toward her at a breakneck speed.

"Must be the soldiers returning to the fort," she said, her head cocked to one side as she waited for them to go past. "Talk about stirring up the dust. Everything in the cabin will be covered with it."

Before the last word left her mouth, she looked up to see an Indian brave riding bareback on one of the horses. The thundering hooves stopped abruptly and the house was surrounded with Indians; their faces painted red so they all looked like demons. They each had either a rifle pointed at her or an arrow drawn back in a tightly strung bow. One arrow was only two feet from her heart and the Indian's eyes didn't look like he was likely to be agreeable to negotiations.

Velvet's temper rose up from the Dulan blood she'd recently found she could rely upon to get her through difficult times. She hadn't ridden a coach from South Carolina, joined a wagon train of brides in St. Jo, Missouri, walked all the way across Nebraska, had a near death experience with fever, and put up with Hoyt Baxter just to stand there and let that Indian shoot her in the heart without saying a word. *What would Willow do?* She thought and discarded the question. Willow wasn't there and Velvet was. *What would Velvet do?* She asked herself.

Grandfather said when all else failed she should pray. Of course, he meant that she should pray to the Father in this instance to receive her spirit into Heaven. But Velvet wasn't ready for that visit with St. Peter. She stared the Indian right in the eyes, wondering why he hadn't shot her yet. She'd heard from Patty O'Leary that any form of fear would surely bring on a fast death. Well, she darn sure wasn't about to let them know her weak legs were trembling under her skirt tails.

She dropped down on her knees, yet never let her eyes leave those of the brave. She tried to look as mean as she could as she began to pray loudly with both hands in the air. Grandfather would drop of a pure apoplexy if he'd seen her. Methodists were a solemn lot and would never make a spectacle of prayer, but Velvet wasn't really praying. She was fighting for her life.

"My God and Father who lives in the sky above the clouds," she said.

The Indian brave looked back at his followers and shook his head. The woman was either crazy or asking for permission into the spirit world. He respected both.

"This Indian is about to shoot me through the heart with his arrow. I will now ask your blessings upon this Indian and his whole tribe. If he lets go of that bow string, I would ask Father that you bless his wife with no children. That if there are children already, that they turn against him and join the white soldiers at the fort to fight against him and his family. If he has a mother, I ask that You bless her with boils upon her body that infect the rest of the tribe. I pray that she will not die but will cry out to her son in anguish, asking him to put an arrow like the one that pierced my heart through her own. And if he kills his own mother, I hope he wanders forever searching for a place in eternity. If he has a father, please bless him with blindness that he cannot see that his son is a murderer of a sick woman who has just recovered from a very bad fever. A fever that will travel through the air from the arrow in my heart to his heart and he will take it back to his camp for all the children and women to die with."

"Hush," the Indian drew back the arrow even tighter. He'd learned the white man's words from his brother who went to a white man's school in Nebraska. He understood every word of the curse the woman was putting on him.

Velvet's eyes never wavered from his. "I ask, oh great Father, that you call down thunder from the Heavens upon this bad Indian's head and strike his friends with lightning."

The Indian heard another brave translating her words in a soft whisper behind him. All of the braves looked up at the small white cloud forming on the horizon in the distance.

"If he ever rides toward into the land owned by Hoyt Baxter again, I want all his teeth to fall out so that he can no longer chew the buffalo meat. And if one arrow hits the window panes of this house which are the blessed eyes in which You can look inside and see that I am living right, then let all these Indians' black hair fall out. Make them bald so their enemies can see that they have angered the great God of the white man. Then let their enemies go to war with them and let their strength be gone even as Samson's was in the Good Book."

"I, Running Antelope, said for you to shut up, you crazy woman. I have spoken. You will die first and then the white man who keeps this land will die and then we will go to the fort and kill all the soldiers," the Indian said.

"Oh Father, if this man kills even one white person, then

take away his name. Let Running Antelope have his legs shot with the soldier's bullets, and get poison in them. Let his women cut them off with the sharp knives. He will die a bald old man with no teeth and no legs. They will no longer call him Running Antelope but they will call him . . ." she searched her mind for something vile enough to rename the Indian. Mercy, but she'd just about used up all the curses she could pray for. Grandfather was probably having a spell even as she spoke.

"They will call him Rat with No Legs. Let all the buffalo meat in his camp rot with flies covering it. Let the children laugh behind his back because he tempted the God of the white man. Let them poke at him with sticks and let his family be ashamed of him."

"I will shoot you if you say another word," Running Antelope said, but the authority in his voice was gone, replaced by a stuttering fear.

"Then shoot me. I'll go to the great Father in the sky and sit next to him. I shall talk to him every day and look down upon your pitiful tribe and I will make sure that I travel on the wind to whisper in the ears of the chief and the tribal council that it was you who brought the seven plagues upon them," she said defiantly.

Plagues. That brought on a whole new idea. "Bring them grasshoppers to eat their corn just for threatening me, Father. And if they aren't out of my sight in the next five minutes then bless them by taking all their firstborn children from them within the next week and give them to white women to raise up in the whiteman ways. All these favors I ask because I am truly Thine own dear child, and I believe with my whole heart that whatever I shall ask, shall be granted unto me."

Quietness filled the yard for a whole minute.

"Shoot me. I have petitioned the God of Heaven and He will be swift to answer my prayers. Put that arrow between my eyes or my heart, Running Antelope, or else get off this land and don't you ever come back," she said.

"I don't believe in your god," he said.

"I don't believe in yours, but if you asked yours for a big favor would he grant it?" She said. "I do believe mine will. So shoot or go home and take care of your end of this land. Just don't you let me see your face here or at the fort again."

The other braves began to talk in some language she didn't understand. Running Antelope snapped the arrow back and tossed it into the quiver. He stared at her long and hard before he raised his arm, yelled something that made the hair on her arms stand straight up, and rode off as fast and furious as he had arrived.

Bummer began to bark when the noise got closer. Hoyt stopped talking to the tombstones and wrinkled his brow. He could feel the thunder of hooves in his knees. It could be either a stampede from a cattle run, or soldiers riding back to the fort. Or it could be a band of renegade Indians looking for trouble. By the time he was on his feet, he could see the horses in the distance. Indians riding bareback straight for his ranch. Rooster Wilson had told him there'd been unrest last time he brought out a load of supplies from the fort. Now, it was here and Velvet was at the house alone. He palmed the fence, jumped it and was in the saddle in less than a minute. The Indians would take great pride in Velvet's scalp, yet even as he rode he remembered his gun was in the cabin and he hadn't even strapped on his pistols.

He rode like the devil was chasing him back to the ranch, only to arrive just in time to see Velvet on her knees; Running Antelope, the renegade who constantly caused trouble at the fort, with an arrow aimed at her heart, and then suddenly just as he brought his horse to a stop, the Indian put the arrow away. Before Hoyt could say a word, he yelled something and the whole pack of them tore out of his yard.

"You have a devil woman," Running Antelope said as he rode past him. "You would do well to throw her in your white man's well, or drive a stake through her heart."

Velvet was sitting in the swing when Hoyt rounded the house, leading his horse. Bummer still growled at the smell of the intruders. "Running Antelope suggests I throw you in a well," he said, swallowing the lump of fear in his throat.

"Well, some men do get irate when the lady of the house says they can't come in for lunch. I'm sorry if they're friends of yours, sir. But that venison roast you put in the oven this morning will not feed that many men. If you've got a mind to ask an army to lunch then you'll have to cook more food. I'm not sharing my portion with a bunch of painted Indians," she said, swallowing the pumpkin-sized lump of fear in her own throat.

"You don't know how lucky you are. That was a war party out for scalps and blood," he said, sitting down on the porch steps, his wildly beating heart still pumping adrenaline into his body in anticipation of an all-out Indian attack.

"I think they've changed their minds," she said sweetly.

"What did you say to them, Velvet?" He asked.

"I didn't say much. I just dropped down on my knees and commenced to praying. I guess they are a religious bunch and didn't like my prayers," she said honestly. "Now about that roast. I do believe if you would allow a woman in your kitchen, I feel well enough to make a blackberry cobbler for dessert to go with it. I saw a couple of jars hiding back behind the green beans on the shelf."

Chapter Five

Hoyt grudgingly admitted to himself that Velvet was indeed a marvelous cook that Thursday night. Gentle night breezes flowed across the porch as he kept a steady motion in the swing and listened to her cleaning up the kitchen. He shut his eyes, planning to pretend Myra was the one washing dishes and taking care of the evening chores while he and Bummer watched the day end. But all he saw was a picture of Velvet with long, brown hair tucked into a bun at the nape of her neck; big, strange colored blue eyes full of life; a tiny waist above the swell of well-rounded hips; more than an ample bosom. He opened his eyes wide and refused to close them again until he had to. He wouldn't see another woman. He would never be unfaithful to Myra.

Velvet's strength wasn't what it had been before the sickness, but she'd pushed herself hard each day, and the results were producing progress. On Monday she'd found him doing laundry when she arose just at the crack of dawn. She'd made breakfast and managed to dust, sweep and mop the floors before she had to sit a spell to rest. By the time he came in that evening from the fields, she had the laundry sprinkled and ready for ironing the next day, as well as supper on the table. Hoyt Baxter wasn't ever going to be able to tell anyone, not even himself, that she hadn't pulled her own weight while she stayed at his cabin. Tuesday morning he found her making breakfast when he came down the staircase. When he finished up the day's work, the ironing was done and supper was on the table. Wednesday, she'd mended everything she could find—even darned his socks—and made three loaves of fresh bread. By Thursday, he'd left whistling and came home in the evening to the aroma of apple pies.

After supper, Hoyt and Bummer sat on the porch while Velvet cleaned the kitchen. In the dwindling daylight, Hoyt contemplated the past week. They'd talked very little. Since the episode with the Indians on Sunday, she'd been quiet, not even asking him any more questions, which suited him just fine. He'd gone about his normal routine and convinced himself that he'd be glad when she was gone.

Suddenly, Bummer raised his head from the porch, sniffed the air and growled.

"Evenin' Doc." Rooster led his pack mule and horse around the end of the porch.

"Wondered why Bummer had his hackles up," Hoyt said. The time had finally arrived. Rooster could take his wagon and haul Velvet and her trunk to the fort tomorrow morning. Hoyt should have been glad, but suddenly it felt like there was a stone weighing down his heart.

"Shoulda known it was me. Been two months, you know. Started to stop on my way in to the fort, but you never change up your order and besides the cabin was all dark so I figured you was sleepin'," Rooster said, tying the mule and his horse to the porch post. "Brought you sugar and flour, couple of them cigars you like and all the old newspapers they'd let me beg, buy, borrow or steal."

"Well, I got me a little problem, Rooster," Hoyt said. "I need you to take it back to the fort tomorrow. Since you'll be going back for me, then I reckon I'll owe you something."

"Nope, I ain't goin' back to the fort. Goin' home tomorrow," Rooster said, a twinkle in his old eyes, set deep on a bed of wrinkles.

"Who are you talking to?" Velvet fanned her face with the tail of her apron as she stepped out of the open door to the porch.

"I'd be Rooster Wilson, ma'am," Rooster said, offering his hand.

She shook it firmly. That was a good thing, Rooster determined. She wasn't a limp wristed, simpering southern belle.

"I'm Velvet Dulan. You had your supper yet, Mr. Wilson?" She asked, a soft southern lilt to her voice.

"No, ma'am, sure ain't," he said. "Where you from? Voice like that got to come from the south."

"South Carolina from birth until a few months ago. Come right on in here and I'll set you up a plate. Got lots of beans and ham leftover, some fried potatoes and a hunk of corn pone. There's a whole apple pie left, so I reckon we can feed you if that sounds acceptable," she said.

"Sounds right fine to this old hermit," Rooster said with a chuckle. "You comin' in here or am I goin' to steal your woman right out from under your nose?" Rooster looked down his crooked nose at Hoyt.

"I'm not his woman," Velvet said bluntly.

"Hmmmm," Rooster pursed his mouth. Best not to push the matter right now, at least not until he'd eaten his fill of that apple pie.

The man didn't come much past her shoulder, she noticed when he limped up the four steps onto the porch. One leg was at least two inches shorter than the other one, causing his whole left side to slope, but his smile was spontaneous and sincere. With a broad sweep of his arm, he practically bowed, letting her enter the house before him like she was royalty.

She took a plate from the shelf and filled it generously with potatoes and beans, added a huge chunk of corn pone and set it before him. While he ate, making appreciative noises, she poured a cup of coffee from the simmering pot on the back of the cook stove.

"You kin to Jake Dulan?" Rooster asked between bites.

"He was my father," Velvet said, questions in her eyes as she cocked her head off to one side.

"Fine man. Best card player in the whole world," Rooster said. "Me and him spent a week snowed in few years back. He'd took one of them wagon trains off to California and weather got him on the way back to St. Jo. Made it to my cabin and holed up with me until the storm passed." He took another bite of ham. "Mighty fine vittles, ma'am. Hoyt'd do well to keep you around. House looks right nice, too. Place needs a woman's touch."

"Then why haven't you got one?" Hoyt barked.

"Why, who'd have an old crippled up hermit like me?" Rooster laughed, mopping up the rest of the bean soup with his bread.

"Pie?" Velvet asked. "Quarter or half?"

"Oh, half anyway," Rooster said. "Ain't often a man gets a real nice apple pie like this. I might even steal the rest of it when I leave tomorrow mornin'."

"Well, you'd be welcome to it, Mr. Wilson. I can always make more. There's apples goin' to waste out there," she said, nodding toward the back door.

Hoyt rolled his eyes. He'd looked forward to having the rest of that pie for his supper tomorrow night . . . after Velvet was gone.

She served it up on a clean plate covered with clotted cream and Rooster shut his eyes reverently while he ate. A man shouldn't talk when he was sitting in heavenly places, and this was about as near ethereal as Rooster ever expected to be.

"Would you tell me about my father?" Velvet asked.

"Be right glad to," Rooster wiped his mouth on a napkin she'd laid beside his plate. "That was the best pie I've ever put in my mouth, Miss Velvet. Which one of them daughters are you? Jake told me he had five girls scattered from Texas to Virginia."

"I'm the one in the middle. From South Carolina. None of us sisters had any idea there were other children until we were called to his death bed. All of us arrived within twenty four hours of each other, only to find he'd already died. We found out there were five of us when Hank produced his will and Rafe Pierce read it to us. None of us ever knew him," she said.

A thousand questions flooded Hoyt's mind, but he wouldn't utter a single one of them. He didn't need to know her life's story. She'd be gone tomorrow morning.

"Well, Jake talked a lot about you girls. Said he'd made five of the biggest mistakes in his life. Told about how he'd fell in love when he was a young man and married up with the lassy. The next year she died having his daughter and he run off. Talked about how that was his first mistake. He shoulda took that baby with him, even if he was young and stupid and didn't know a thing about no girl babies."

"That'd be Gussie," Velvet said, nodding. She clung to his every word.

"Yep, that's right," Rooster said as he patted his stomach. "Then he told me about four more little girls whose mothers up and died, one way or the other . . . all except the last one. He laughed when he said that there came a day when he and that little girl's mother just figured out they plain didn't like each other. Kid had a strange name, but then all of you girls do, don't you?"

"Yes, Augusta. We call her Gussie, then Garnet, and me,

and Gypsy Rose and Willow. Willow fell in love with Rafe Pierce and they got married a few weeks ago. She's gone to his ranch in Nebraska to live. The rest of them are on a wagon train," she explained.

"On that fool mission of Hanks to take them women out there to California to marry them gold diggers?" Rooster grinned.

"Yes, that's the one," Velvet nodded.

"Well, if that don't beat all. I'd feel sorry for them men, gettin' daughters of old Jake Dulans. Why if they had an ounce of his temper and a pound of his stubbornness, them men is in for a lifetime of surprises," Rooster said.

"They just might be, at that," Velvet smiled.

Lord, but she was a beautiful woman when she smiled, Hoyt thought, then got angry with himself for even thinking like that. Myra's memory didn't deserve such thoughts.

"Well, that's about all I know about your Pa, girly. I'm right sorry he died and you didn't get to know him none. He was quite a man. But I'm glad I got to meet up with one of them girls he talked about that week. Kinda makes the story of them and their mothers come to life." Rooster sat back in his chair. "Now, how about me and you take us a cigar to the barn and have us a smoke before old Rooster finds him a hollow in the hay mow?" Rooster asked Hoyt.

"You can smoke in the house. I grew up in South Carolina. Tobacco country, you know," Velvet said.

"No ma'am. Rooster Wilson ain't smoking in a house this clean and leavin' the smell of tobaccy on your pretty curtains. Besides I got this name, Rooster, because I go to bed with the chickens and get up before they do," he chuckled. "Come on Hoyt. Humor me a little. Won't see me no more until the spring thaw. I'm takin' enough supplies home to keep me through the winter snows."

Hoyt followed him out to the barn, where they both sat in the dirt and propped their backs against the open doors.

Velvet could see them out the back window as she cleaned the dishes and put them away. The bright red glow of the cigar's tips looked a bit out of place with the twinkling stars and rising moon. Every now and then, the night breeze brought her a little sniff of the smoke, and with it memories of her childhood home.

Grandfather was a preacher in the United Methodist Church in Brattensville, South Carolina. It had been his fondest wish that Velvet's mother would attend the Brattensville Female Seminary and when she eloped with the worthless Jake Dulan, Grandfather had come close to losing his mind, according to Grandmother. Jake wasn't nothing but a foreman in one of the tobacco sheds. Grandmother never let Velvet forget it, either. She could still hear her grandmother's high pitched voice telling her she should be thankful she had kin willing to take her in and raise her when her father had proven his worth. Grandmother said she just hoped Velvet didn't grow up to be as worthless as Jake Dulan or as flighty as her mother.

When her mother died and Jake left her in the care of her grandparents, she supposed he thought he was doing what was best for her, but Velvet would never forgive him. Not for the life he sentenced her to; the hours on her knees praying that she wouldn't grow up to be like her father; the loveless home she grew up in; the deacon her grandfather tried to force her to marry. None of it. Not even if he did tell Rooster he'd made at least five mistakes in his lifetime when he didn't take his daughters with him.

He'd left her to a life of not much more than a slave. Hoyt Baxter didn't know how close he'd come to the real story when he said Velvet was a slave's name, or how much she'd wanted to be a slave when she was younger. Grandfather didn't actually own slaves—on paper. But he didn't have to officially own them. The richest of his congregation made sure their slaves took care of the good preacher man. A vision of the cook and cleaning lady who came every other day to the manse slipped easily into Velvet's memory. Lizzy and her daughter, Mandy, a beautiful little girl with skin only barely darker than Velvet's, in the kitchen humming as they worked.

"Velvet, now you and Mandy, get over there and roll out that dough for some sugar cookies," Miss Lizzy had said more than once, and the girls giggled and played while they made big round cookies sprinkled with sugar. At least until that last day, when Velvet announced at the supper table that she wished she could go and live with Lizzy.

Grandfather had choked on a piece of Lizzy's lemon cream pie, and Grandmother wrung her napkin nervously.

"Why would a little white girl say something like that?" Grandfather demanded in his big booming preacher's voice.

"Because I could play every day with Mandy and Lizzy loves me like I was her own. She told me so. And I don't know why anyone would ever want to own anyone and make them do work like they do Lizzy and Mandy. They're just like us, Grandfather. The only difference is that their skin is darker and that isn't a sin, is it? I wish my skin was black as that old gardener's skin that Mr. Rubenstein sends us on Thursday. I'd rather be a slave than an orphan with no mother and a daddy who was just a foreman at the tobacco sheds. At least someone would love me."

That little speech reaped her a whole hour of begging for forgiveness on her knees, along with ten lashes with Grandfather's belt. It was right next door to blasphemy to wish things like that, he'd declared. She was supposed to be praying for grace, but instead she had prayed that someday she'd be rich enough to buy Lizzy and Mandy. She'd set them free and they'd adopt her for their own family. God didn't hear her prayers. Two days later a big, overweight woman came to cook and clean. She wore a rag tied to her head and Velvet was terrified of her. Velvet never saw Lizzy or Mandy again, nor did she feel that soft, warm, fuzzy feeling in her chest when they hugged her tightly just before they left every day.

Just before Velvet got on the stage coach to leave town, Bessie, the woman who cleaned and cooked, showed up. She handed Velvet a basket with sandwiches inside and smashed Velvet's face into her big bosom. "Don't be blamin' yourself, child. Lizzy married up with the butler over on the next plantation and they bought her and Mandy long years ago. Mandy is done married and a momma twice over now. She's a maid in the big house. Didn' know nothin' 'bout that bizness what went on in your house 'til a little bit ago. Heard your old grandpappy tellin' that deacon how he'd taught you to mind yore manners when you was a little child. I'm glad you're goin. Don' come back here. Ain't nothin' for you in this place."

"I won't Bessie," she whispered. "I won't ever come back."

Another whiff of sweet smoke penetrated through the night air and into the house. Someday, Velvet swore, she was going to smoke a cigar just to see if they did indeed taste as good as they smelled. The soft droning of masculine voices joined the aroma but she didn't care what they were talking about. It had been a long day and her eyes were heavy. Hoyt knew the way to his own bed and Rooster would sleep in the hay mow. She didn't need to bid either of them a good night.

"I wouldn't take that lassy to the fort, even if you give me the deed to this ranch," Rooster said after they'd sat a while.

"And why's that?" Hoyt's dream vanished into the night air, carried away on the wings of a lightning bug. The woman wasn't leaving tomorrow and he didn't like the feeling that idea brought. It wasn't justice to Myra, and he couldn't tolerate anything that disrespected the memory of his wife.

"Well, right now the general over there wants to rent her, Hoyt. Says he'd pay any amount you want to have her stand up on the top of the fort and bring down the lightning if Running Antelope gets an itch to fight agin. The Indians revere her. Think she's got some kind of potent magic. But the women folk over at the fort, well they just plumb hate her. They're all speculatin' as to how she's out here livin' with you and that ain't right in their self-righteous eyes," Rooster said.

"And how'd they even know she was here? I'd just thought you could take her to the fort and pretend you brought her in. Make up one of your tall tales," Hoyt said before blowing a perfect smoke ring. By closing one eye and cocking his head slightly to the left he could see the moon through it.

Rooster chuckled. "You don't know what went on out here last Sunday?"

"I was up at the cemetery for my weekly visit and a war party came up. By the time I got here Running Antelope was fuming. Told me I should toss the woman in the white man's well," Hoyt said.

"What did she tell you happened?" Rooster asked.

"Said they got upset because she wouldn't invite them in to supper or something like that. I just figured they were afraid of the fever and took off like scalded dogs when they saw how weak she was from that fever," Hoyt answered.

"Well the way of it was like this. The general has got him a spy that watches the tribe and when he saw Running Antelope and his braves getting ready for a war storm he came high tailin' it back to the fort to warn them. They loaded up the big guns and posted soldiers all over the fort. Put the women in safe keeping and all. Then they waited, only it never happened. The spy nearly lost his good name 'til he found out the next day what happened," Rooster began drawing out the story. It was just too blamed good to rush through and although the moon was high, the night was still young.

"She did what?" Hoyt exclaimed when he'd heard the whole thing.

"Yep, she dropped down on her knees and brought down the curses in the form of blessins upon his head. Ain't an Indian in the tribe who would've gone to war that day, superstitious as they are. Who wants to be known as Rat with No Legs, or to have all their black hair fall out. And that ain't even mentionin' boils on his mother's body." Rooster held his ribs in laughter.

"What's that got to do with the women at the fort?" Hoyt bit the inside of his lip but the grin split his face anyway.

"That's a different story. They ain't havin' none of her "lifestyle" as Opal called it amongst them. Opal says if she wants to live out here in wanton sin with you, well, that there's her own business, but she ain't bringin' it in to the fort for them to have to look at," Rooster said.

"Clara, too?" Hoyt asked.

"Clara most of all. She's married up with one of the soldiers there," Rooster said. "Guess you didn't know or you wouldn't have dropped that cigar on the ground. Done looks like she swallowed a watermelon. Opal's the one who stirred up the other women the most of all but Clara followed right behind her," Rooster said, shaking his head.

"But Clara said she'd never marry. She'd wear black forever for Boyd," Hoyt said.

"Well, this mornin' she was wearing a pink hatchin' jacket. And one of them soldier boys was leadin' her around by the elbow. Reckon the lady done changed her mind, Hoyt. Comes a time when you bury the past and the dead and get on with the livin'. Can't blame Clara none. She loved Boyd and he loved her, but she's young and Boyd's dead," Rooster said. Wasn't no need to beat around the bush about the thing. Hoyt might not like it, but Rooster wasn't dressing up his words just to please Hoyt.

Hoyt sat there a long time, digesting all of what Rooster had said. Velvet, protecting his ranch and him, bowing up to the Indians when most women would have fainted dead away. Not one of the eleven at the fort, including Opal and Clara, could have done that. Those women had no right to judge her and if he hadn't made a vow never to set foot inside that fort again once he brought his brother's body out, he would go there and tell them just what a lady they had judged so wrongly. Not a single one of them would have pushed themselves the way Velvet had done these past days. Working hours past exhaustion when by all rights she could have laid in bed all day.

Not even Myra? His conscience nagged.

"I'm going in to bed, Rooster. Guess I'll see you when the thaw comes in the spring time," he said, ignoring that nagging inner voice. Myra was a saint of the purest kind and he'd never compare her to any other woman—including the spunky, sassy Velvet Dulan.

"Yep, guess you will. If you got a lick of sense you'll still have that woman in there when I come back," Rooster said.

"Never been accused of having good sense," Hoyt said, patting his old friend on the shoulder. *If I had good sense, I wouldn't have walked out of Ft. Laramie last year. I wouldn't have let my brother talk me into doing something that I knew down in my bones would kill him. But I did and it did.*

Velvet heard the door close softly and the third step squeak as Hoyt made his way up the stairs to the loft. Next week she would move her things up there—as soon as she could carry that chest without falling back down the stairs with it on top of her. She'd simply unload it, carry her things up a bit at a time and then drag the trunk up. Seemed only fitting now that she was almost well that she give his room back. Yes, maybe on Monday, she'd attempt the move. That would be a good day since the sheets would be off the beds for wash day.

The moon all but filled her window for a few minutes, shining through the lacy curtains and making a pattern of light and dark on the top of her sheets.

"In the beginning God created . . ." she recited aloud from the Bible. She kept whispering the familiar verses until she got to the one she wanted. ". . . and the evening and the morning were the first day."

So there, she thought. *That settles it. The evening was first, and then the light of day followed. The moon dawns and the sun rises. First comes the experiences of night followed by the light of day. Darkness first; light second. I'm progressing through the night toward the light. Although I know I'm in the night, I'm afraid to leave it because the light scares me. What's there, Lord? What's in the light for me? I'm afraid, so please just let me have the night even with its problems a little longer. I'm not ready for the light of day.*

Hoyt fought with his pillow, plumping it, then flattening it. He shut his eyes so tight that they ached, but sleep didn't come. Finally, he laced his fingers on his chest and watched the stars out the loft window. A cool night breeze blew across his body while the night frogs joined forces with the crickets and a lone coyote to provide one of nature's operas.

He'd met Myra at an opera in Baton Rouge and had fallen desperately in love with her at first sight. The daughter of a general, she knew all about military life and was more than ready to go west with him to Fort Laramie. The perfect wife in every aspect. That was his Myra.

Bury the past and get on with the livin'. Rooster's words bounced off the rafters above him. No, he wouldn't bury the past and he wouldn't get on with the living. His life ended a year ago; his body just didn't know it yet.

Chapter Six

Velvet made up her mind Saturday night that she was going to church on Sunday morning. Hoyt would go wherever he went every Sunday and she'd never be missed. As if he'd care where she went or if she ever came back. It was time she went to the fort and made acquaintances. There was a possibility she could work for one of the families there until another wagon train came through the country. She'd gladly work for room and board. There might even be the outside chance there was a small school at the fort and she could teach at it until such time as she could book passage with another train. Anything to be away from Dr. Hoyt Baxter's ranch since he'd made it as plain as the snout on a boar's face that he didn't want her there, especially since she'd grown strong enough to be deemed cured from whatever fever almost killed her.

Hoyt had been especially gruff ever since Rooster came and went. Whatever bit him on the posterior had produced an old bear and Velvet was eager to be away from the ranch for a little while, possibly forever. He'd told her that the fort was a little less than two miles south once before. She

figured she could walk that in forty five minutes and services usually began sometime around ten o'clock.

He finished his breakfast and picked up his Bible like he
did on previous Sundays and read for the exact number of
minutes. Velvet wondered if there was something in the
Good Book she'd missed. Something that said, "Thou shalt
sit in the same rocking chair every Sunday morning and
read thy Bible for exactly this amount of time or thy soul
shall suffer forever in hell's fire." Her grandfather would
have her sitting on a chair facing the wall contemplating
her horrid sin of thinking thoughts like that, or else married
off to a deacon old enough to be her father.

When he disappeared out the back door, Velvet opened
her trunk, took out her best dark blue dress, the one she'd
worn to her father's funeral, and a slat bonnet made of the
same fabric, trimmed in white lace to match the trim on
the collar of the dress. She dressed carefully. This would
be the first time she'd meet the people, especially the ladies
at the fort, and first impressions were almighty important.
She laced up her walking boots, a little sorry that she
couldn't wear her better Sunday shoes, but her feet would
be screaming in agony if she walked two miles to church
and two miles back home in shoes with such high heels.
She fluffed out the full skirts over her petticoats and decided if she kept her feet covered, no one would ever know
she was wearing brown walking boots.

Bible in hand, she set off at a steady pace, sun rays
sneaking past the brim of her bonnet and warming her face.
A slow smile twitched the corners of her full mouth and a
giggle erupted. She was actually taking charge of her own
life for the second time. The first was when she defied her
grandparents and boarded that stage coach for St. Joseph,
Missouri. After that, she'd actually just gone along with
her four sisters when they wanted to join the wagon train

of brides going to California. Gussie, Garnet, Gypsy and Willow were such strong woman and she'd wished for part of that determination and strength. Well, she'd found it all right. It had taken a near death experience and Hoyt Baxter's sheer hatefulness, but she'd finally found her backbone and she liked the feeling of being her own boss. Nothing could go wrong. Velvet was on her way to church and if there was one place she knew like the back of her hand, it was church. She'd sat in the front pew beside her grandmother all of her life.

She was amazed at the size of the fort when she could see all the adobe walls, complete with a walkway around the top and an overhang above the gates. She'd expected wood poles sharpened on the top, but then the Patee House in St. Joseph, Missouri had surprised her, too. There, she'd expected at best a two story ramshackle hotel, not a huge brick building holding more than a hundred rooms.

"State your business, ma'am," the sentry said when she reached the gate.

"I'm Velvet Dulan and I'm here to attend Sunday morning services," she said.

"You're the woman who's living with Dr. Hoyt Baxter?" He grinned a bit too familiar to suit Velvet.

"I'm the woman who Dr. Hoyt Baxter healed from a fever a few weeks ago," she said. "I am staying temporarily at his cabin until I can find employment elsewhere. Now are you going to let me go inside the fort to the services or have I walked two miles in vain?"

"Sassy, ain't you? But then I'd expect that from what I've heard about you. And when you find a place for that employment, you let me be the first to know," the sentry said. "Go right on in, Miss Dulan. Don't know just what kind of reception you're going to get. Us men folks would like to kiss your feet, but the women, now that's a different thing."

"Whatever are you talking about?" Velvet frowned, a cold chill of dread tickling her backbone in spite of the summer morning's warmth.

"Oh, I think you know very well," the sentry said with a wink. "Enjoy the services. The chapel is at the far end of the fort. Little building with a cross on the top. Too bad you didn't send someone to let us know you'd be here this morning. The soldiers would be standing ten deep to get a sight of you."

"Why?" Violet was really beginning to get worried.

The soldier just laughed and waved her on through.

She found the chapel easy enough and was the first one inside the doors. Out of habit she chose a seat on the front pew, then had second thoughts and took a seat at the very back of the chapel, sliding all the way to the end. She opened her Bible to the twenty third Psalm and began to read quietly while she waited. In a few minutes, other people began to arrive; a few soldiers, the chaplain who eyed her curiously, and exactly eleven women, one of whom was very pregnant.

"I see we have a guest," the chaplain said when he took his place behind the podium at the front of the small chapel.

Velvet looked up to find a room full of eyes staring right at her. She wanted nothing more than to wiggle in embarrassment like she'd done when she was a small child and someone noticed her. So much for that backbone of iron she'd been so smug about.

"Please stand up and introduce yourself." The chaplain said, motioning with his hand. "Has one of the officers brought a new wife and not told us?"

She took a deep breath, remembered her sisters telling her that her Dulan blood would stand her in good stead when she needed it, and hoped they were right. She stood gracefully. "No, I'm not a new wife. I'm just Velvet Dulan. Dr. Hoyt Baxter has been kind enough to doctor me back to health after a horrible illness," she said in a soft southern voice and sat back down.

Soldiers stared at her with twinkles in their eyes and smiles on their faces. The women were a different matter. Not a single one of them smiled; they looked more like they'd just stepped in something a horse left behind and were wondering how to shake it off their boots. If looks were capable of killing, Velvet would keel over and breathe no more. The ladies stared their fill, then as if on cue, snapped around, sat ramrod straight and looked up.

Velvet sang the hymns from memory in a fine soprano voice but when the chaplain began his message, her mind wandered. What on earth had she done to bring the wrath of those women down upon her head? And how'd they know her anyway? An hour later, when the preacher finished his sermon, the soldiers all gathered round her to welcome her to the fort and asked her to come back again. Evidently, the jitters were just the effects of walking into a new place without knowing anyone. She'd overreacted, she told herself as she joined the rush of men out into the church yard.

"So you are Velvet Dulan?" An older lady with mousy brown hair and the same shade eyes pointed a finger. "Well, I'm not afraid to stand up and speak for the ladies who have to live inside these walls. There's eleven of us, and you are not welcome here, Velvet. Go on back to Hoyt Baxter and live in sin with him. I can't believe you'd show your face amongst decent women."

"You don't know what you're talking about," Velvet said, a slow hot blush lighting up her cheeks. "I was about dead and one of the wagon train crew brought me to Dr. Baxter. He was kind enough to heal me. I'll be leaving as soon as I can find a job or as soon as another train comes through. I'm on my way to California."

"Sure." The woman laughed in her face. "Hoyt Baxter

doesn't practice medicine anymore. Not since he killed his brother and his wife. There is no way he would take up medicine again. Not with some stranger when he's refused to even doctor his best friends. I don't know what cow patty you crawled out from under but you won't find a job or a welcome here in Fort Laramie, and you are a fool if you think you will. If you want to live out there with him, that's up to you and him. But we loved Myra and we won't be forgiving him, and we sure won't ever condone what he's doing with you. Stay away from our church and our fort. That's an order."

"Sorry, darlin'," Velvet said softly even though she wanted to slap the woman all the way into next week. "I don't belong to the U.S. Military so I don't have to take orders from you or anyone else at this place. When God tells me I can't sit on the back pew in there and worship then I won't come back. Good day, ladies." She slipped her bonnet on her head and tied the ribbons under her chin. With her back as straight as a sober southern judge, she walked away from them, right through a pocket of soldiers who'd listened to the conversation, and who were receiving a severe dressing down from the head lady general of the fort. The poor soldiers probably felt like tucking their tails between their legs and slinking off to the bar for a double shot of whatever was left over from Saturday night. Velvet would have bet her Bible that most of them wouldn't show up next Sunday for services if that's the blessing they received afterwards.

Hoyt bent low over the tombstones he'd carved from wood and brushed the dust from the names. He needed to tell them about his week but somehow the words wouldn't come. He couldn't tell them about Velvet or about Rooster's story, much less about the way she cooked his meals, washed his clothing and took care of the cabin. It wouldn't be right to tell all those things, not when they made it sound like he was enjoying Velvet's company. He surely did not want the woman in his house, he kept saying over and over in his heart, but standing there in the little graveyard, he wondered who he was trying to convince. Them or himself? She sure couldn't tell Boyd that Clara hadn't even mourned a whole year. She'd married within weeks and was expecting the baby that should have been his, not some other greenhorn soldier's.

His tormented soul lay heavy in his chest as he led his horse back to the ranch. If only she'd leave on her own. Just disappear as suddenly as she had showed up in his bed that day. He sat down on the porch and put his forehead in his hands, resting his elbows on his knees and ignoring Bummer. The seams of his neat little world had begun to crack and he didn't like losing control one single bit.

He'd put off going in and looking at Velvet long enough. He had no doubt that she was in there, reading her Bible as she rocked back and forth in Myra's favorite chair. He'd been an old bear all weekend, and that pricked his pride. He hadn't been raised to be curt, snide and meaner than a hungry swamp gater. But then there was nothing in his raising that prepared him for the past year, either.

The front door swung open to a house as empty as his heart. Everything was in place, but there was no Velvet. Hoyt's first thought was to shout. She'd gone and his life could go back to whatever warped normalcy he desired. Then the shell of a heart beating in his big broad chest crumbled. She was gone and he didn't want his sorrowful life back. Completely opposite forces fought within his spirit: one demanding that he go find her, the other reminding him emphatically of his vow to remain true to Myra for the rest of his life.

He sat down in the rocking chair and tried to sort out the emotional battlefield. He shut his eyes and prayed for peace but apparently God said no, because the turmoil did not cease. Maybe Rooster had realized that Velvet would be better off at the fort instead of living with Hoyt and had returned to haul her back there when he knew Hoyt would be out tending to his Sunday duties. If that was the case, she could have left him a note, at least. A thank you for saving her life wouldn't have been completely out of line.

Sure, and she'll thank you for your sweet attitude when you did it. Besides she's worked like a slave around here since she's been well. She's more than paid you back for what you did, he argued silently.

The bedroom door stood wide open so he wandered in there in hopes there would be a letter on the pillow or propped up on the chest of drawers. But there was nothing. Nothing but her trunk, which meant she hadn't left for good. A wide smile spread out across his face but he felt guilty for it.

She must be in the barn or out gathering eggs. Still undecided about how he truly felt, and still thinking he had some say in what his heart should do, he crossed the back yard and slipped into the barn. The barn cat was there with a nest of five new mewing kittens hid back in the last stall.

But there was no Velvet.

His eyes drew down in a frown. Surely Running Antelope hadn't come back and kidnapped her right off the front porch. Cold sweat broke out on his forehead. The renegade brave might think he would inherit her spunky spirit if he took her scalp. It would be quite a coup for him to declare that he had captured her magic for his own. That painted-up Indian didn't know fury if he'd harmed Velvet. She was Hoyt's responsibility while she lived under his roof and if Running Antelope wanted a battle, then Hoyt would take him a full-fledged war.

Bummer yipped out in the yard and Hoyt saw the black-and-brown streak when he dashed past the barn doors.

Probably Rooster coming back with the news that he now needed her trunk since the women at the fort had a change of heart once they got to know Velvet. Why wouldn't they? She was a sweet natured woman with an iron will, was extremely determined, hard working, a good cook; he could go on and on listing her good qualities.

He peeked out the barn doors to see Velvet stop long enough to rub Bummer's ears and then go into the house. He breathed a heavy sigh and hurried across the yard. He opened the back door at the same time she opened the front one. If Running Antelope had kidnapped her, he'd sure raised her ire to the boiling point. Those strange aqua blue eyes were fairly well afire with anger. For a second, he wondered if Running Antelope was still breathing or if his name had changed this morning into Rat with No Legs. The only thing she had in her hands was her worn black Bible but Hoyt didn't have a doubt that she could have taken Running Antelope's legs off at the knees with that if she had a mind to.

"What are you looking at?" She stomped into the kitchen and jerked her bonnet from her head.

He'd never seen that dress before. It was a lovely blue one that accentuated her narrow waist and rounded hips. "Where have you been?" He asked, hoping the worry didn't come through his words.

"You go where you want on Sundays and I don't ask questions," she said, tossing her bonnet onto the rocking chair. She sat down at the end of the table and raised the hem of her dress to pull off her boots.

Walking boots. Not dress shoes. And petticoats. Her ankles were trim and neat, her feet small for a woman of her height. He'd forgotten how provocative a woman's ankles could be, and swallowed hard in his dry mouth.

"Fair enough," he said.

"I went to church at the fort," she said. If he wasn't going to fight about it, then she didn't care if he knew. What she wanted was a good rousting fight. She should have gone against her raising and knocked the hatefullness right out of that spiteful woman. A good old rousting, hair-pulling, biting fight with them rolling in the dirt and screaming ugly words at each other. Not unlike the one she'd witnessed as a teenager when two girls in South Carolina fell in love with the same boy. It seemed so hoyden that day when she watched them make utter idiots of themselves. But right then her fingers itched to yank hair and her feet wanted nothing more than to kick.

"You walked to the fort?" He asked.

"Well, you didn't see me unsaddling a horse or parking a buggy did you?" She snapped. Men! Did they think they were the only ones capable of walking a couple of miles to and from Sunday morning Mass?

"Did you see any of the women who live there?" He asked cautiously.

"Why are you asking?" She eyed him coldly. He didn't look like someone who could kill his wife and brother. There was sadness in his big, dark eyes and it was evident there was a mental load on his shoulders, but murder? She didn't think so.

"Well, well . . ." he squirmed a bit, wondering how much he should tell her.

"Well what, Dr. Hoyt Baxter? Why did you ask me that question?"

"Rooster said that the women there are up in arms about you living here unchaperoned," he said all in a rush.

"And you didn't tell me?" She raised her voice an octave and her dark eyebrows even farther. "You let me walk into that lion's den without a word?"

"Hey, you didn't tell me you were going to church. You didn't say a word about walking into the fort. I might have told you if I'd known," he defended himself.

"Sure you would have," she said.

"What happened?" He asked.

"Since you've had two whole days to know about the way the fort felt about me, and you've been a bear both of those days, hardly saying a word to me, then I'll be sent to the gallows before I tell you anything," she said, slamming the bedroom door in his face.

With jerking movements born out of rage, she unbuttoned her dress and shoved it off her shoulders, pushing her petticoats down with it. She kicked it aside and threw herself down on the bed, wiping tears of frustration away with the back of her hand. Those women had no right to publicly humiliate her. If they didn't want her in their midst, they could have simply sent one lady to talk quietly to her about the immorality of living with a man without a chaperon. Well, they'd left her no recourse. She wouldn't run from them. No siree, she would not.

Next Sunday morning she'd be sitting in the very front pew of that church. And if they didn't like it, then, like the men in the bars said, they'd "take it outside." And she'd give them a little dose of Dulan temper. She wasn't that meek and mild little girl who received a whipping for wishing she was a slave, and she surely wasn't the same Velvet Jane Dulan who'd used her father's sickness as an excuse to get away from a potential husband more than twice her age. She was beginning to find herself in this dark world and by the time the light came around, there might not be a single person around who liked her, but she'd be able to look in the mirror and live with the woman looking back.

She wiped the last of the tears away, stood up with determination, and reached for her calico day dress. She had a whole week before next Sunday and there was work to be done. She'd shed enough tears for a beautiful Sunday morning ripped to shreds. She might as well fill Hoyt in if she had to stay there longer.

Hoyt's eyes stared at the bedroom door for a full minute. What had those shrewish women said to her? Finding out would mean a trip back into the fort and he'd vowed he wouldn't go back there. Not when he'd made an error that cost him his twin's life. He wasn't fit to be a doctor or an officer. He'd just have to weasel it out of Velvet—someway, somehow.

The door swung open as violently as it had been shut and she stood before him. "They said I wasn't welcome in their church and I wasn't ever to come back there," Velvet began. "The men treated me like I was some kind of queen. I guess it's because they think I'm living out here in sin with you and I might be up for sale to the highest bidder when you get tired of me. Matter of fact, the sentinel at the gate said that when I found other employment to let him be the first to know. Now I know what he was talking about."

"Oh, and what do you intend to do?" He bit the inside of his jaw to keep from smiling. Somehow a grin right then might get him the back side of her hand planted firmly on his face.

"Well, since it's not ladylike to fight, especially right after listening to a Sunday morning sermon, I postponed the hair-pulling contest until next week. We're having fried venison for lunch with gravy and biscuits. You got a problem with that?" She threw over her shoulder as she made her way to the kitchen.

"If I did, I sure wouldn't voice it right now," he muttered.

"You're smarter than I figured," she said.

"You going to tell them you're just here like in a hospital?" He was so close behind her she could feel his breath on the tender skin at the nape of her neck. Shivers brought goose bumps on her arms and down her back.

"I told them that and they didn't believe me so I'm not

telling them anything else. Gypsy Rose says when someone says something ugly and you jump out there and defend yourself, well, it's like stirring in a cow patty. Just makes it stink the worst. I already tried to explain and the stink rose up over half the state of Wyoming. No, next week, I'm not saying nothing. I'm just going to church and if they don't stay out of my way, then they can suffer the consequences."

"Which are?" He asked.

"For someone who hasn't talked to me all weekend, who's sulked and pouted around here like a spoiled child, you sure do have a lot of questions," she said, stirring flour and milk for biscuits.

"I have not acted like a spoiled child," he retorted.

"A rotten to the core, spoiled child," she said, her nose inches from his. What would it be like to kiss Hoyt Baxter, she wondered, then felt a slow blush creeping into her cheeks.

"I'm going outside," he said slowly, trying to regain his balance. He'd come within a half an inch of leaning forward and claiming those pretty lips for his own. Talk about adultery in the purest form. He couldn't kiss Velvet. He wouldn't kiss any woman ever again.

"That's a good place for you," she said. "But before you go, tell me just what it was you did that makes those witchy women think you murdered your wife and brother?"

"That's none of your business," he said curtly.

Well, I'll make it my business, Dr. Hoyt Baxter she thought as she beat out her exasperation with a wooden spoon and a bowl of biscuit dough. *If I've got the name of a harlot by living here in this house with you, then I'll make it my business.*

Chapter Seven

The bed sheets flapped gently in the Monday morning breeze. Violet scrubbed the rest of the laundry, attempting to work out the frustrations that robbed her of a night's rest. From the time her mother died, she hadn't been a wanted child, so what made this situation so very different? The ladies at the fort had stood behind their she-cat general and made it plain they didn't want her. The fact that Hoyt didn't want her couldn't be made any clearer.

"Well," she said, wiping the sweat from her brow. "Hoyt is just one man and a surly one at that. But living with one man even if he doesn't want me here is nothing compared to eleven women and more than two hundred men. That's how many are there according to what Hank said when he determined the wagon train didn't need to stop. Gypsy said it was because he didn't want to loose another woman or two to those soldiers."

"Who are you talking to?" Hoyt asked.

"What are you doing back here already?" She snapped at him. How much had he heard of her tirade? She wondered. He never came back until lunch time and sometimes

71

not even then, so what was he doing here startling her like that?

"Forgot something." He whistled as went into the barn and rode off again with some kind of metal device in his hand. "Oh, forgot to tell you," he yelled back. "There's a new batch of kittens in that empty back stall. Thought you might like to take a look."

Would wonders never cease? He'd actually said something nice. She dried her hands on her apron, left the mop rags in the bottom of the wash tub to soak and went off in search of the new born baby kittens. The last time she'd held a baby kitten was when Mandy brought one in with Lizzy. Grandmother came close to having the vapors when Mandy brought it in the house. According to Grandmother, there would be cat hair everywhere and probably some kind of dread diseases to go along with it. Why everyone knew if a child swallowed a cat hair it gave them worms. Velvet was enough of a problem to raise in a preacher's house without her becoming ill, Grandmother reminded her emphatically. The cat had to go in the back yard. Velvet and Mandy played with it all day and strange enough, Velvet stayed healthy.

Velvet found the nest just where Hoyt said and sat down in the straw beside them. The mother cat purred and Velvet felt the same sound in her own heart. She reached out and picked up the yellow one. It wasn't nearly as fluffy as the one she and Mandy had played with, nor was it as big, but it would be someday. She counted five wiggling babies; the yellow one, two black and whites, a calico and a solid black one.

All five of them were hers.

Sure, they are, something inside Velvet said. *You'll be leaving on the next train headed west and those kittens will stay right here. No wagon master is going to let you bring five cats along on a trip like that.*

"They're mine as long as I'm here anyway," she declared, picking up one at a time and nuzzling them into her neck. "And there just might be a wagon master who'd let me take at least one of them," she said on the way back to the washing tubs.

Dark clouds formed on the far horizon just as she finished up the washing. She shaded her eyes with the back of her hand and hoped they were slow moving and her laundry would dry before the storm came. She'd just have to keep an eye on it and make haste to bring the clothing in before it hit or else she'd have to do it all over again tomorrow.

The next job for the day was to put a pot of beans on to boil and then she fully well intended to move her belongings to the loft. If she had to stay here in this unwelcome house then she would at least give Hoyt back his bedroom. Besides, truth be known, she wasn't comfortable in there with a dead woman's things laid out on the chest of drawers as if she would be returning any minute. Whatever the story was concerning all that, it wasn't natural for Hoyt to hang on to the past like a bull dog with a bone. However, that was his problem. Velvet was simply going to do what she could to repay him for her room and board and stay out of his way as much as possible.

A narrow circular stairway led up to the lion's lair where she'd never set foot before that day. Going up there empty handed would be a waste of energy, so she gathered an arm full of clothing from her trunk, and set off to a new adventure, even if it was simply moving from one part of the house to the other. She unloaded the burden on the bare mattress of a narrow bed and took stock of her new home.

She'd have to take the extra clothing he had hanging on a rope stretched between two rafters back down with her when she went for the second load. The bed was half the size of the one she'd been sleeping in, but it still beat sleeping on a bedroll underneath a covered wagon. No curtains flapped in the morning breeze in the one window that opened in the same direction as the one down stairs. Good. That way she could watch the dawning of the moon each night.

Taking his things from the line, she made her way back down the steps to transfer more things. She noticed that the dark clouds still hung back as if afraid they'd bring down the wrath of a Dulan if they ventured into her territory too rapidly.

Four trips up the stairs later she finally had the roll top trunk unloaded and all of Hoyt's things on the bed in his room. She'd have to make the bed shortly when the sheets dried but she hated to open the armoire to do so. She'd never swung those doors open, figuring what was inside it or the chest of drawers was none of her business. Still, she had to put his things somewhere, or else leave the bed unmade. Sucking in a lung full of air and bravery—after all who knew what monsters might lurk behind closed doors—she gingerly eased the doors open. Lavender scent rushed out into the room. She cocked her head to one side and simply looked at the pretty dresses for a few minutes, then reached out and touched them reverently. Myra had been a small woman, not any bigger than her sister, Gypsy Rose, and she favored pinks.

That she'd been loved desperately was no secret. Hoyt had left everything in the room just like it was before she died. To know that kind of love, Velvet crushed one dark pink smock to her face and inhaled deeply of the lavender scent, would be the most wonderful thing in the world. An undying, unconditional love. Monogamy at its epitome. Once married, always married. Never to part, not even after death.

She sighed deeply and realized what kind of garment she was holding. Why, it was the kind of smock women wore when they were expecting a baby. She gave in to curiosity and thumbed through the rest of Myra's things. Several flowing tops hung beside the dresses with tiny waistlines. So there had been a child before Myra died. Where was it? Was it a boy or girl? And, more important, who had it? Was Hoyt Baxter just another Jake Dulan? Was his daughter living with some grandmother who hated the job of raising her?

Taking two steps backward, she sat down on the bed with a plop. So that was why he'd been so cross after Rooster came and went. Rooster had told that story of how Jake regretted his decision to leave his children in the care of other people. Well, she hoped it seared his conscience, making it burn for weeks. The scoundrel. How could a man love a woman so much and then forsake the child they made together? He wasn't any better than a common tom cat. Make babies and then run off to the next sand box to play a while. In the space of a few minutes, Velvet Jane Dulan decided she was not going to Bryte, California to marry a gold miner. There wasn't enough gold in the whole state to convince her to do that. No, she'd made up her mind. She was going back to Nebraska to live with her younger sister, Willow. She'd be an old maid school teacher or a governess or she'd work for Willow and Rafe on the ranch, but she'd never marry.

Not ever.

By the time she dragged the empty trunk up the steps she was exhausted. She stretched out on the bed and took several deep breaths, reminding herself that she had the worst of the day finished. Then she smelled the sickening, rancid odor of burning beans. She jumped up, banging her head on the sloped ceiling and hurried to the kitchen. Not only were they burned, but they'd stuck to the bottom of the kettle which meant it would have to soak and Hoyt would know she'd been careless. She grabbed a hot pad and hoisted the cast iron kettle off the stove, hauled it outside to the pig pen and poured it into the feeding trough, adding a little water to cool the stinking mess so the pigs wouldn't burn their mouths.

She made a side trip to the spring house and picked up the back haunch of venison, reminding herself that they needed to use the meat by tomorrow or it would ruin. As she poured water into the iron kettle from the wooden bucket Hoyt had filled that morning from the well, she fussed at herself again for being careless.

She peeped out the kitchen window at the storm clouds. They looked serious, close enough now that she could smell the rain through the open window. She'd just take time to slice off three thick steaks for lunch and a nice, big roast for supper, and then she'd gather the clothes in. Leftover roast would make lovely sandwiches tomorrow for lunch. There was a silver lining in every dark cloud. Burned beans meant she had to work a little harder today but it made tomorrow's load lighter.

The first raindrops hit with a vengeance just as she took the last full basket into the house. Big, round drops blew through the open windows. Hastily, she removed the props and shut the windows and remade the bed in Hoyt's room. The quicker she could be out of there and away from its reminders of the woman's spirit who still slept with him, the better she'd like it.

She peeled a pan of potatoes, putting some on to boil for lunch, and saving the others back for roast. Declaring she wouldn't forget the potatoes like she had the beans, she gathered up her own clean laundry, along with the sheets for the loft bed, and carried them upstairs. Careful not to bump her head even once, she stretched the bottom sheet tight, folding the corners perfectly just like Lizzy had taught her and Mandy to do all those years ago. She'd just fanned the top sheet out when she heard the back door open. Well, the old bear had more sense than she gave him credit for. He'd at least come in out of the rain.

Hoyt shook the water from his hair, not totally unlike Bummer did huddled under the swing in the semi-dryness of the front porch. A black pot with water standing in it did nothing for his already gloomy mood at being caught out in the rain without a slicker. Now there wouldn't be a hot lunch, either. Miserably wet, he took the steps two at a time, and ran smack-dab into Velvet at the top.

"What are you doing in my room?" He growled, pushing her away from him, yet deep down wanting to draw her back into his arms.

"It is no longer your room, Dr. Baxter, but mine," she said, hoping her silly heart didn't beat so hard that it popped the buttons off her dress.

"It's my house, Velvet Dulan. I'll make those kind of decisions." He narrowed his eyes and glared at her.

Instead of intimidating her, she began to laugh. An old wet bear, acting like he had a sore tooth and an ingrown toenail, coming into her bedroom and telling her what kind of decisions he would make.

"Don't you laugh at me!" he shouted. Holy smoke, he hadn't raised his voice like that in so long he made his throat ache. Why, the last time he'd been that angry was when he shook his fist at the sky after Boyd died, and screamed until he had no voice for a solid week.

"I changed rooms with you today so you could be back in there to wallow in your precious past." She sauntered up to him until her nose was only an inch his, her mouth so close that it almost made her forget her vow to never marry. "So just chase your wet self back down those stairs and you'll find all your things right back where they belong. Clean sheets on your bed and everything put in order. I won't disturb your sanctuary anymore."

He continued to glare at her. "Get out of my house," he finally whispered.

"Sorry, Lord Baxter," she said. "You see, I have no where to go just yet, but I'll promise you one thing. As soon as any kind of traveling mode comes through here going to Nebraska, I shall beg, borrow, steal or buy a ride on it."

"California, not Nebraska. Your mail-order husband is waiting in California," he argued. How dare she defy his order! It was his house and she had no right to make decisions in it.

"No, Lord Baxter." She drew out the sarcastic title she'd just bequeathed on him. "Nebraska. I've decided to live with my sister and be an old maid. Men like you and Jake Dulan should be shot, but that's against the law. Having children and not even caring what happens to them. Letting them grow up in a world with little love and made to feel like even being a slave would be better than . . ." She stopped before the tears that were welling up in her eyes flowed down her cheeks. She wouldn't let him see her cry and have the satisfaction of knowing he'd pushed her that far.

"Not all men are like that," he said.

"You're one to talk. Now you'd best get back down there and change out of your wet clothing before I have to take care of a man with pneumonia. I might not be as kind as you were. I might just let you die," she said curtly. The fight was over. Even Hoyt Baxter, with his good looks and drawing power wasn't worth arguing with any longer. "Besides, I've got potatoes boiling to mash for lunch. We're having venison steaks, gravy and biscuits. I'll cook a roast for supper. And after supper I'm thinking about canning a few jars of meat so we don't waste the rest of that venison."

His stomach growled. Two huge meals in one day. That might make up for the fact he'd be confined to the house all afternoon with that shrew of a woman who took matters into her own hands. No, he wouldn't spend the day with Velvet. He'd go to the barn and muck out all the stalls, rub oil into the tack, even play with the kittens. Anything would beat watching her gloat because she won the battle of the rooms. Well, one battle didn't mean the war, and he would have her out of his house before long, even if he had to pay someone to carry her all the way to Nebraska on their backs.

He shot her one more mean look, bumped his head as he turned around and started back down the spiral staircase with her right behind him, smelling for all the world like lavender. He regretted the day he'd given her Myra's cake of scented soap. Now every time she was within three feet of him, he remembered Myra smelling just like that.

He was on the bottom step when he felt a whoosh of wind born from rustling petticoats and the scrap of her boots when she missed a step. He turned in time to see her arms flailing. Her body drove him backwards, down the last step. The momentum took them both to the floor; Hoyt, flat on his back, staring at the ceiling with the wind knocked plumb out of him; Velvet, stretched out on top of him, her skirt tails up around her neck, making a tent for both of them from the waist up.

Hoyt mentally checked his bones. None were broken. Then he opened his eyes to find the clearest blue ones in the whole state of Wyoming staring at him blankly. It was as if they were asking, "How did I get here?"

"Oh, my," she finally gasped. "Are you hurt?"

"No, you?" He whispered, his breath warm on that tender part of her neck, right below her ear.

"I don't think so," she said.

He flipped her skirt tail over her back. Then, he rolled over, wrapping his arms around her to cushion her body against the hard wood floor, and suddenly her eyes were even closer. "You sure you're not hurt?" He asked hoarsely.

"I don't think so," she said in a far-away voice. She liked the feel of his heart beating in unison with hers; liked the tingles playing tag up and down her arms where he touched her; liked the way her neck felt, still warm with his breath; liked the wild beating of her heart. No, she wasn't physically hurt, not at all, but suddenly Velvet Dulan grieved for something she could never have.

She pasted on a smile. *Make light of the whole thing and don't let him know how bad this encounter has rattled your reserve*, she thought. "Well, now wouldn't the ladies at the fort just love to walk through that door right now?" she said, arighting herself into a sitting position and carefully covering her ankles and petticoats.

Hoyt pushed himself into a sitting position and then stood to his feet. The turmoil boiling around in his heart produced only a blacker mood, but he'd be a gentleman and help her up. He offered a hand and she took it, the tingles of her touch almost burning his skin. The infidelity toward his wife's memory was burning his conscience just as badly.

She was trying to stand up gracefully when her feet slipped on the wet floor he'd left behind. He barely caught her before she fell right back onto the stairs which she'd just fallen down. He pulled her to his chest to steady her balance. One minute he was busy keeping her from a second fall, the next his hands were around her slim waist and his mouth was on hers for a long, demanding kiss that rocked both of their rainy worlds to the core.

It lasted for an eternity, yet it was over in seconds. He released her, turned his back abruptly and stormed downstairs into his bedroom, slamming the door behind him. Lord, what had he just done? He had relinquished all the vows he'd made the day they buried his sweet wife.

He'd been unfaithful, and she wasn't even here to fight with him about it. He threw off his wet garments and dug around in the chest of drawers for a clean union suit. Then he opened the armoire doors. The scent of lavender met him and the sight of her clothing humbled him.

"I am so sorry, Myra. It won't happen again," he promised, hugging one his favorite of her dresses to his chest.

Velvet stood there in stunned silence for the longest time, the warmth of his kiss still lingering on her mouth, her own vows to never love a man shattered in a million pieces around her feet. What would she do when he came out of that room? How did one handle a situation like this? Nothing in her background prepared her for that. She shook her head. It had all been a mistake. He hadn't really meant to kiss her. She wouldn't have let him if she hadn't fallen and knocked her senses out into the rainy day. The only practical thing to do was forget it happened. Go on with the day's business and simply pretend it was part of a crazy dream.

It would be easy. Just go into the kitchen and prepare lunch. When the door to the bedroom opened, pretend he was coming in from the fields for the mid-day meal. She got a skillet and put it on the stove, adding a big spoon of lard. Then she drained the potato water in a bowl to mix with cream for gravy. The lard had just reached the right temperature and the steaks were sizzling when he opened the bedroom door.

He picked a book from the mantle and sat down in the rocking chair. Acting as if nothing had happened was his policy, too. Velvet could read whatever she wanted into that kiss, but it would never happen again. She'd be gone before long and someday he'd forget about the way his heart soared and his body reacted to her lips on his. He pretended to read, keeping his eyes downcast and the book only inches from his nose, but in reality he watched her deft movements as she prepared lunch. There was a lucky man waiting in Nebraska for Velvet Dulan. She'd make him a fine wife, in spite of her resolve to be an old-maid school teacher. No woman with lips that kissable and a body that yielding was destined to be an old maid. No, she'd find the right man and they'd settle down in the rolling hills of Nebraska and have a full life. His heart twisted into a knot thinking about another man holding her like that and tasting the sweetness he'd just partaken of. But he would not—could not—be untrue to Myra.

Velvet mashed the potatoes and turned the steaks, sizzling in the hot lard. She slipped a pan of biscuits in the oven, and tried her best to ignore Hoyt, sitting in all his self-righteous martyrdom. Would anyone rip at his heart strings the way he'd just done hers? She hoped so, and when they did, she hoped that he'd bury all his guilty past, whatever it was. No one, not even a mean old bear like him, deserved to live his best years wrapped up in robes of self-condemnation. Evidently, he hadn't really murdered his wife or his brother, or he would be behind bars, not running a ranch outside of Fort Laramie. Something horrible must have happened, and everyone seemed to make sure he took the blame upon his shoulders. He had left it there for far too long, Velvet thought.

"Lunch is ready," she said finally, amazed that her voice sounded normal.

He laid his book aside and took his place at the head of the table. "Would you please say grace?" He asked, bowing his head and shutting his eyes tightly. He wasn't worthy at that moment to even approach God with thanks for a well-prepared meal.

"Of course," she said.

When she'd finished, he raised his head to find her staring right into his eyes. His resolve almost melted, but he took a deep breath and asked her to please pass the gravy.

"Don't whip yourself," she said as her fingers grazed his when she handed him the bowl. "It was only a kiss. Nothing special. Just a kiss. It just happened. We can just forget it."

Maybe you can, he thought. *But it's tearing my heart apart. One piece wants to forget everything and drag you to the rocking chair, into my lap and kiss you until I've had my fill. The other wants to spend the afternoon on my knees in front of that open armoire begging forgiveness for my wanton desires.*

"You are right. That's what we'll do. Now could I have some biscuits?" He reached, but he was very careful not to touch her fingertips.

She nodded.

Of course I am, she ate without looking up. *It's the right thing to do, even if it isn't what's really in my heart. Even if just looking at you in your socks makes me want more of those kisses, just to see if the whole world lights up in a bright array of beautiful colors every time your lips touch mine.*

Chapter Eight

Velvet opened the trunk, which she had shoved under the sloped eaves of the roof in the attic to give her a little more space. Careful not to bump her head, she brought out a clean but faded blue floral shirt waist and matching skirt. She found her oldest slat bonnet and laid all of the clothes on the bed. Today, she was going to work in the flower beds. They'd been let go until they were an absolute disgrace. Weeds overtook the lantana and the marigolds needed thinning, not to mention the disheveled disgrace the roses were in.

It seemed as if she and Hoyt had reached an unvoiced agreement to disagree since Monday. Being back in his own bedroom hadn't sweetened his attitude one bit, but then sleeping in the loft hadn't made her the happy woman she'd thought it would, either. Her reputation was in shambles and moving out of his cabin wouldn't repair the damage, so she'd do just as well to stay put. The reception at the fort would be a disaster with the men thinking she was a common harlot and the women's opinion being even lower than that. At least Hoyt hadn't completely thrown her out—yet. Fastening the last of the twenty small buttons up the front of her dress, she figured it wouldn't be long until he did, though.

Out of habit she checked her reflection in the tiny mirror he had hanging right beside the door. Yes, the same old Velvet looked back at her. She hadn't grown horns or a wart on the end of her nose. She really wasn't a witch, so why did those pious, perfect women want to burn her at the stake.

She had her bonnet in her hand when something in the back of the room caught her attention. She'd lived up there most of the week and had never noticed that dark object pushed back into the far reaches of the attic.

"Now what is that?" she wondered out loud. She sat down on the edge of the bed and eyed it for a while, knowing full well it wasn't one bit of her business. If it had been meant for anyone to see, then it wouldn't have a dark covering; however, curiosity wasn't something that Velvet was able to control. She leaned forward, wrinkled her brow and tried to figure out what it might be. It was too short to be a chair; too small to be another bed; too big to be a wood box. It couldn't be a special thing belonging to Myra because all her belongings were still in the shrine Hoyt called a bedroom. So what could it be? In moments she was across the room, tugging on one side of the heavy, black material. The fabric fell away to reveal a lovely, rocking cradle made of burled oak. She sat down beside it, running her fingers over the hard wood. The inside of the cradle was filled with baby things: Soft, nappy diapers were sewn with the neatest hand stitches she'd ever seen. The lovely little gowns had perfect little button holes and embroidery around the hems. Several bonnets with lace and frills and a couple of very plain ones with blue ribbons. A whole layette of things Myra must have made when she wore those smocks in the armoire.

"He didn't even send them with the baby when he sent

it away," she muttered, a tear dropping off her long, dark brown lashes onto her cheeks. "The child won't know that its mother loved it so much because it will never see any of these beautiful things."

The time had come, she decided as she carefully redraped the cradle. Hoyt Baxter was going to answer some questions as well as stand still for a big chunk of her mind. She was about to get right in the middle of his business, whether he liked it or not. If she accomplished nothing else with this stay in his house, she was going to make him understand that he needed to bring his child home and give it the love of one parent. He could hire one of the women at the fort to come and help him with it through the day. At least the little thing would know his care and attention in the evenings. Boy or girl, it could go to school at the fort and play with the kittens in the barn when it got big enough to toddle out there.

Flowers forgotten, she donned her bonnet and stormed out the front room door. This wasn't waiting for Hoyt to come home for lunch. No, sir. She was taking it right out into whatever field he was in right now. She marched with determination to the edge of the yard and then realized she had no idea where he was during the day. He ate his breakfast in tense silence and then he and Bummer left. He always came home with dirt under his nails that he had to clean with his pocket knife before he sat down to eat. If he wasn't coming for lunch, then he simply didn't show up. She never knew where he went or how long he was staying.

She stood there in utter bewilderment. How much land did he own anyway? And which part of it would he be on today? Which way should she start out? There was a trail that led off to the north that appeared to be well traveled so she decided to start with that one. She shoved her hands into the deep pockets of her skirt and began walking, agitation mounting with each step along the way.

Fifteen minutes and a dozen revised sermons later the trail ended at the edge of a copse of oak trees. In the middle of the grove she found a small cemetery surrounded by a white picket fence. Sun rays broke through the dense oak foliage in a few places and the shadows dulled the brilliance of the white fence. Everything about the place said she wasn't welcome. The trees, acting like valiant sentinels, protected the graves inside the fence. The sharply pointed planks forming the fence seemed to be saying, "Go away. This is private." The gate itself, closed to anyone who found the little place, told her that she should mind her own business and go look for Hoyt somewhere else.

Undaunted, she swung open the gate and went inside, in spite of the silent warnings. She'd come this far and she wasn't leaving until she'd seen who was buried in such a beautiful, well-kept place. Could this be the place where he went every Sunday morning?

Three tombstones were lined up perfectly, the history written for her to read in precious few words. She began with the first one, touching each wooden cross reverently.

Myra Mason Baxter; June 5, 1839–June 1, 1860. Beloved wife of Hoyt Baxter.

Weston Mason Baxter, June 1, 1860–June 1, 1860. Beloved son of Hoyt Baxter.

Boyd Wesley Baxter, August 21, 1832–June 8, 1860. Beloved twin brother of Hoyt Baxter.

It took several moments for what she read to soak in but when it did she dropped to her knees, tears flowing down her cheeks unabashedly. Myra had died along with her son on the day she gave birth to him the year before, probably of complications. That's why the cradle and its contents had never been used. Not because Hoyt had sent his child off to be raised by relatives but because he'd buried his wife and baby on the same day. That's why the cradle was draped, so he wouldn't have to look at it every night he climbed those stairs. A fresh wave of guilt washed over Velvet. No wonder he was still melancholy, and then to bury his brother exactly a week later—his twin brother at that. It was a pure miracle that he wasn't stark raving mad with the grief of it all.

She absentmindedly pulled a lonely weed from the base of Myra's tombstone. "He loves you so much, Myra," she said between soft sobs.

"What are you doing here?" Hoyt shouted from his horse before the animal even stopped. He literally hit the ground running, jerked open the gate and pointed outside, demanding that she leave, too angry that she'd invaded his privacy. Not one person had ever set foot in this place since the day they buried his brother. That day he put up the fence and the gate in, and it had become his own special shrine to the three people he'd loved the most. She had no right to go poking her nose into places where it wasn't welcome and surely did not belong.

"Don't you dare!" she shouted right back at him, standing up and approaching him with such force that he dropped his hand. Forget about pitying the man. Grief hadn't only depressed the man, it had turned him just plumb mean.

"Get out, Velvet. I don't share this place with anyone. It's . . ." He stopped mid-sentence when she was just inches from him.

"It's what, Hoyt? Your own haven of martyrdom? It's a cemetery and I can come here and grieve if I want to. You don't have a monopoly on grief, you know," she said.

"You don't even know them. Never did and never will. You aren't grieving for them. You're just satisfying your morbid curiosity. Well, I won't have it," he said hoarsely.

"No, I didn't know them," she said. "But I can imagine

her carrying that baby for nine months, only to loose it and then breathing her last. I can imagine what that must be like, Hoyt. To leave behind a person like you who loved her so much he still can't even let go of the past and get on with life. I can imagine her lying there trying to hang on to the last thread of life just so she wouldn't disappoint you after she'd already lost the baby you wanted so badly. I don't know what happened to your brother but it can't have been easy for you to give him up the very next week, either. So I can mourn if I want to. I can do it, not out of morbid curiosity, but because I'm a woman and there's not a blessed thing you can do about it."

"You don't know nothing." His jaw muscles worked and his teeth stayed clenched as he spoke.

"No, it's you who doesn't know anything. That woman had to have loved you enough to want you to go on with life, Hoyt. You are a disappointment to her, acting like this. I'm going back home now. You can do whatever you want. Wipe all the defilement from the gate if you want. I touched it, you know. You might want to take off your shirt and clean the tombstones, too, because I touched them. Goodness knows you can't have anyone else sharing your grief. Oh, no, you want to keep it all for yourself so it can rot your insides. I'm going upstairs to my room and you'd better not even knock on it. I'll come out when I'm ready. You can get your own lunch, too, or you can stay right here and wallow in your own self-pity. Right now I don't care what you do." She accentuated every word of her last sentence with a push on his chest.

Before he could answer she'd marched out of the gate, slamming it back with enough force to make the fence tremble. Hoyt waited until she was out of sight then he dropped down on his knees at the end of his wife's grave. "I'm so sorry, Myra," he began. "I told you about her and her violent temper last Sunday. I wish she'd just go away and never come back most of the time. Then others, I wish she would stay. I don't know what to do, Myra. I love you so much and I made a vow after I lost you and the baby. Only now, I'm confused and I don't know how to handle it."

A gentle breeze blew softly across his tear-stained face but no answers came with the wind. It was something Hoyt Baxter would have to figure out for himself and then live with his decision. Myra had been gone for a year now, along with the baby and his brother. He had only their memories to sustain him, and lately, it seemed like they were failing desperately.

Velvet threw herself on the narrow cot and let the tears, both of anguish and anger, flow down her cheeks. Hoyt would come storming through the door in a little while, demanding that she get her things together and get off his property. That much was a positive fact. Where on earth she'd go was another matter. Stage coaches didn't run every day, and Fort Laramie didn't want her to dirty their streets until one did chance through that area. She wiped a tear and wondered briefly just how far Rooster lived from this place. He'd welcome her, she was sure, and would be much better company than Hoyt. If he'd teach her, she could even learn to play cards to keep him entertained.

Bummer's yipping said the inevitable was close at hand. Boots on the wooden front porch said it was drawing nearer. The squeak of the third step brought it even closer. At least he wasn't stomping, so the eviction notice wasn't going to be in a fit of rage, but a stone cold order. Either way, it would bring about the same results.

To her astonishment, he knocked ever so gently on the door instead of plowing right in.

"Come in," she said, barely above a whisper, sitting up

on the bed and wiping her cheeks with the back of her hand.

He didn't look at her as he sat down on the other end of the bed, keeping his eyes on the toes of his dusty boots. "I owe you both an apology and an explanation," he said, hoarsely. "Myra and I were only married three months when she got pregnant but we were ecstatic. I'm a doctor. I knew she was too small to bear the child naturally, but she was afraid of surgery, and then there's the chance that if she had the baby that way, she'd never be able for another one and she wanted a big family."

"You don't have to do this, Hoyt," Velvet reached across the space and took his hand in hers, patting it gently. "I was out of line."

"No, I do need to do this," he said. "Not only so you'll understand but to get it out of my chest. It's weighing me down and killing me slowly. I thought I didn't want to live, Velvet. I was just waiting out my time until I could go and be with her and the baby in eternity, but lately it seems she's telling me that's not what is right."

She entwined her fingers in his and waited.

"Anyway, I kept telling her we needed to go to the Fort and put her under sedation and let me take the baby, but she refused. That kind of birth can bring about it's own problems and to tell the truth I was scared to try it on Myra so I probably didn't beg her hard enough. Besides she cried buckets and made me promise no matter what happened I wouldn't do that. She was so afraid she'd never wake up. Well, I listened to her and my son was too big. Stillborn with the cord wrapped twice around his neck, and then I lost her, too, within an hour." His voice was emotionless, as if he were relating a story that had happened to someone else. "I was lost. Myra was my whole world and she was gone. We buried her. Boyd and I dug the graves ourselves. The chaplain came out from the fort and had the service.

Two days later, I was sitting on the front porch in a limbo world, not caring if I lived or died when a messenger came riding up saying that Boyd had fallen off his horse and broken his leg. I raced to the fort. The break was right above the knee and the bone was sticking out of the flesh a good inch. His leg needed to come off but he threw a fit. How would he support his fiancé, Clara, with no leg. No, I was a magician. I could set it, sew up the wound and he'd be fine. He didn't care if he walked with a limp, he kept saying. I argued. Threw a real fit right there while he was suffering, but he said before I put him under that if he awoke with his leg gone, he'd hate me the rest of his life. I did what he asked. Gangrene set in and he was dead three days later. I'm not fit to be a doctor. Scarcely fit to be a man, because I let my personal life interfere with what I knew was medically best."

She waited, holding tight to his hand.

"I buried my brother beside them in a private ceremony. Me and Rooster. Forbid any of the fort to come out here. Not even Clara. She didn't want to come anyway. Blamed me for the whole thing and rightly so. Said she could have lived with a one legged man better than a dead man. I walked out of the fort that day behind the wagon bringing my brother's body out here. I've never been back. Won't ever go back. I've been numb for a year now. Rooster says when I get over being numb, I'll get angry. I think I reached that part today at the cemetery. Everything is void now. I don't know what to do with it, Velvet."

She slid across the bed and drew his head down to her shoulder. "I'm so sorry," she said softly into his dark hair. "It isn't your fault. You can't make a person lie still for surgery. You're not God, Hoyt, but just a man. Don't whip yourself because you abided by their wishes. If Myra had been another man's wife, could you have forced her to have that baby surgically rather than the way nature intended? I don't think so. You might have begged and told her the consequences if complications arose, but it would have been beyond your reach to force her. Same with Boyd."

"Rooster said the same thing. I didn't believe him, either," he drew back from her. He wanted to stay there forever in the circle of her arms, drawing comfort from the warmth of her breath as she talked with that soft southern drawl, but it wasn't right. Words were, after all, just words, and they couldn't erase what he'd done.

"You will believe it. Someday, you will Hoyt, and the day you do, is the day you'll begin to live again," she said, finally letting go of his hand.

"Thank you for not . . ." he searched for the right words. For not condemning him. For not screaming out that he was a complete fool and unworthy to be a doctor, like Clara had done.

"Let's go on down to lunch," she stood up so fast that she bumped her head on the rafters so hard that it made her dizzy. She fell back on the bed, one hand holding the growing goose egg on top of her head, the other stifling the sobs. Lord, nothing had hurt that bad since she'd fallen out off the back step when she was a child and knocked herself silly on a rock beside the porch.

"What have you done?" Hoyt kneeled beside the bed and removed her hand from the edge of her hairline at the top of her forehead. "Mercy me, but that's going to be sore for a few days, to say nothing of the black and blue bruise it'll produce. But at least it's protruding to the outside. If something that big had gone inside you would have had a concussion."

He leaned forward to get a better look at the knot and suddenly his dark eyes locked with her light blue ones still producing tears. "Here," he pulled a handkerchief from his pocket and gently wiped away the tears.

"Thank you," she smiled.

Her smile was like sun rays fighting their way through the storm clouds and shining down upon the earth in the middle of a rain storm. Velvet Dulan was a lovely, wise lady as well as being pretty, but when she smiled like that she was truly beautiful. The smile disappeared when his mouth found hers in a crushing, soul-searching kiss that made her even more dizzy than the bump on her head.

"Well, I told you so," a voice said from the doorway. "You are a fool, Clara, to take up for the lies of this wanton woman. Like I said, she'd just as well work in a brothel for what she's doing. It's one and the same in God's eyes."

"What are you doing here?" Hoyt jumped to his feet, barely avoiding knocking himself on the low rafter.

"Came to prove to Clara that this woman isn't an innocent little sick lamb like she pretended to be. The door was standing open and we heard her whimpering up here so we just came up the stairs. If you hadn't been so busy making love with her, you would have heard us," Opal said, hatred glittering in her face.

"Get out," he pointed. "This isn't any of your business and I don't have to explain anything to either of you."

"You go on," Clara said. "I'm staying here awhile, Opal. I think Hoyt will hitch up his wagon and bring me back to the fort in a while."

"You are a fool. Always have been. Fell for that devil, Boyd, and then for one not much better when you married Cyrus. I'm going back to the fort, and don't you ever cross me again," Opal told Clara through clenched teeth. "I'm right. Just like always."

"Maybe so Opal. But I'm not so sure. And until I prove things for myself, I don't care what you say," Clara said.

"I could have Cyrus and you both sent to the far reaches of the world. All I have to do is tell the general you are being ugly to me," Opal argued.

"Go right ahead. The far reaches of the world might be nice if you aren't there," Clara said.

Opal shot her another mean look and flounced down the stairs.

"I've come to apologize to both of you," Clara sat down on the end of the bed. "First to you, Hoyt. I was so mad, I had to blame someone, and Boyd was dead so I couldn't fight with him. Cyrus has told me time and time again it wasn't the right spirit to have. Boyd made the decision to try to keep his leg, and it cost him his life. Wasn't nothing you could do about that. But it had to have been a terrible thing for you right after Myra and the baby. So I'm sorry for the things I said that day when you took Boyd's body out of the fort."

Hoyt nodded, mixed emotions playing havoc with his heart. Opal would waste no time in spreading the news of the condition she'd caught them in. Not that it made a bit of difference to him, but Velvet's reputation would really be ruined now, and suddenly he did care about that. She was a good woman and she deserved more than what she'd gotten since she'd arrived at his cabin.

"And to you, Miss Dulan. I let Opal make the decision to be mean and I didn't stand up to her last Sunday. I can see from that knot on your head, you've just had a nasty accident. What goes on between you and Hoyt is your business, not mine, but I do want to tell you I'm sorry for being weak. I should've stepped up and told Opal she was judging by her own half bushel and didn't know anything about you." Clara patted Velvet's hand. "Anyway, that's what I came to say. Now Hoyt if you'll be so kind as to drive me back to the fort. I'm hardly in the condition to walk that far. The baby is due in three weeks. I won't ask you to go in the gates but you can let me out there."

Clara had blond hair, big brown eyes and skin as fair as any proper southern belle Velvet had ever seen. But for some reason her touch reminded Velvet of Mandy's when she'd been a small child. Honest. Forthright.

"You are forgiven, but only if stay for lunch with us," Velvet said. "I'd love a little company."

"Why, I'd be glad to, if that's all right with you, Hoyt?" Clara looked up at the man who used to be her brother-in-law, the man who was the very image of her first love. She was glad to realize that she really had buried that part of the past; that Cyrus had filled her heart with so much kindness and love that Boyd was just a wonderful memory.

"It's fine with me. Velvet is a wonderful cook, and she could use a friend," Hoyt made his way out the door and down the stairs, leaving the women together, sitting on the bed—much like he'd done a thousand times before in the other bedroom. Clara and Myra, with their heads together, planning a wedding and a baby. The recollection should have been a vexatious weight to him, but somehow his heart felt lighter than it had in more than a year. He went to the barn to try to make some kind of remote sense of all his feelings while Velvet prepared lunch.

"Thank you," Velvet sat up slowly, making sure the dizzy spell had passed. "I do need a friend. I'm afraid I got used to more than a hundred women around to visit with. Not to mention four sisters. A friend would be very nice."

"Four sisters!" Clara exclaimed. "I only had two old mean brothers. I would have loved to have four sisters when I was growing up."

"So would I," Velvet grinned. "But I didn't get them until a few months ago. Come downstairs with me and I'll be glad to share the story, if you'll tell me a bit about yourself."

"Sounds good to me," Clara said, supporting her back as she rose.

A friend, Velvet sighed. One who'd just stood up for her in the midst of a disaster. She could scarcely believe her good fortune.

Chapter Nine

From a vantage point in the hay loft, Hoyt watched Clara's buggy arrive on Friday morning. Later he'd take his wagon out to the backside of the property and load it with wood he'd chopped all week. Fall would soon push out what little bit of summer was left with a few good hard frosts, then before anyone could blink twice winter would arrive in all its bitterly cold glory. Yes, sir, it would be cold in Wyoming before too many months and he would be prepared. Already, two stalls of the barn were filled to capacity with wood, but that wouldn't last out the long, bitterly cold season. The two previous winters he'd used three times that much and Rooster had told him when he came by that this winter was going to be worse by far than any the Fort had ever seen. He could tell it in his bones, he'd said. Whether Rooster was right or wrong, Hoyt intended to be prepared.

Also, by the end of the next week the cattle drivers should be coming through. He'd culled the cattle he didn't want to feed until spring, but he needed to look them all over again to be sure he'd made the right decisions.

When the buggy arrived he forgot about cattle and wood.

He peeped around the corner at Clara, clumsily crawling out of the carriage. Velvet had actually asked him if she could invite Clara for a soap making day. Asked, politely too, rather than going ahead with her plans in his house without considering his feelings. He'd gruffly told her he didn't care what she did while he was out of the house, but he did. He wanted to sit in the rocking chair, pretend to read a book, and listen to female chatter. He'd hated it when Myra was alive; all that talk about how much of this or that, and whether to wear a pink dress or blue one to church on Sunday. But today, he wanted to listen. Wisdom told him it wasn't the chatter he wanted to hear, but Myra's voice amongst it, and that wasn't his to have.

To his surprise, Clara brought Joy Callaway with her. Joy had been Myra's best friend from the fort. By the end of the day, Velvet would be so tired of Myra this, Myra that, Myra did it this way, that's Myra's favorite bowl, that she'd be hauling that trunk to California or Nebraska, wherever she'd decided to go today, on her back just to get away from it all. Joy wouldn't ever let it rest, and poor old Velvet was about to find out all about Myra, whether she wanted to hear it or not. He waited until the ladies were in the house, hitched up his plowing team of horses to the wagon, threw the ax and splitting maul into the back and went to take care of men's work. By nightfall, the whole house would smell like lavender and he wouldn't be able to sleep for the memories.

"Come right in," Velvet opened the door for the ladies.

"I brought along a helper," Clara said. "Hope you don't mind. This is Joy Callaway. She's been at the fort about two years. She's not showing yet, but her first is due in about four months."

"Well, congratulations, Joy," Velvet said, beaming. "I'm glad to make your acquaintance. You two ready to get started?"

"We sure are," Joy said. She'd come prepared to give Velvet a difficult day, but the woman's smile was absolutely heart warming. Clara had said Velvet was a genuine, honest woman and she truly believed nothing was going on between her and Hoyt. Joy surely did not believe her, but then she didn't think everything Opal said was pure gospel either, so she'd come to satisfy her own curiosity.

"Good. Care for a cup of coffee and a sugar cookie before we start?" Velvet asked.

"Yes, ma'am," Clara nodded. "I don't turn down cookies, ever."

"Me, too," Joy added. "Black coffee. No sugar or cream for me."

"Both for me," Clara said. "Lots of both. Make my coffee half cream and two spoons of sugar, please. I'm going to be very unladylike and dip my cookies."

"Where's Hoyt?" Joy asked.

"Off doing whatever it is that ranching men do during the day," Velvet said. "He eats his breakfast and disappears. Sometimes he shows up for lunch. Sometimes not until supper. I never know until he walks through the back door."

"Myra would have his scalp for that. He could at least tell you if he'll be home for lunch so you'll know how to prepare," Joy said.

"Well, she had the right to have his scalp," Velvet said. "Me, I'm just an orphan patient. Left on his bed without his consent and he can't get rid of me. Opal would tar and feather me, then give me to Running Antelope to use for shooting practice if I tried to live at the fort. I do what I can to keep his house clean, his laundry done and meals cooked, but I'm not a wife or even a potential wife, Joy, so he doesn't owe me anything."

"He owes you kindness," Joy said.

"No, he really doesn't. You see, I'm not even a hired hand. Like I said, I'm just here because I have no other place to be. I should've gone home with Rooster Wilson. I think he might be happier to have me around," Velvet laughed.

"By now you wouldn't have any ears," Clara giggled. "He would talk them right off the sides of your head."

"Did you know Myra?" Velvet looked right at Joy.

Joy squirmed. "Yes," she finally answered honestly. "Myra was my best friend. We grew up together in Louisiana and I married a soldier a year before she and Hoyt married. It was my party where she met Hoyt."

"Well, imagine that. It is a small world even out here in the wilderness of Wyoming," Velvet said. "You must tell me all about her. I've lived among her things for so long and know so little about her. Sometimes I can almost feel her presence in this house, telling me not to be too rough on Hoyt."

"That wouldn't be Myra," Joy laughed. "She'd be telling you to kick his rear end out in the front yard for the way he's moping around. She wouldn't like that. She wasn't very big but she had a temper and it surfaced right often!"

"Somehow I figured she was one of those simpering southern belles," Velvet sipped her coffee and picked up another cookie.

"Not Myra. She was a southern belle all right. From down in the southern tip of Louisiana, but sugar, she could hold her own. She could even back down Opal," Clara said.

"Whew!" Velvet rolled her eyes in mock admiration. "Now that I would have liked to see."

"It was a worthy sight to see," Joy agreed. Myra would have liked this Velvet Dulan. Clara had been right. She was genuine and honest.

"Okay, let's get busy or we won't have a single bar of soap to harden when our day is done. Cyrus is so happy to have me out here making soap he could shout. I've moaned and groaned about not having scented soap until he's ready to string me up. You know how some women crave food? Not me, I've craved the smell of Louisiana swamp water and the smell of good rose soap. Didn't know how to make it until you mentioned it the other day when I was out here," Clara said, pushing back from the table and standing awkwardly to her feet.

"You go sit in that rocker," Velvet said, pointing to the smaller of the two chairs that she'd turned to face the kitchen. A soft pillow was tucked in the seat to provide support for Clara's back, and a footstool in front for her to prop her feet on. "You're here to watch the process and learn, not help. I'm glad you brought Joy with you, though, because it would be a hard task to shave soap and stir, too."

"Just show me what to do," Joy said, brushing cookie crumbs from the front of her yellow calico dress, and tucking a strand of bright red hair into the bun at the nape of her neck. "I'm afraid Clara came from a rich family and is as spoiled as I am. Neither of us know a thing about making soap."

"Well, how in the world did all this good soap get made out here?" Velvet asked. "I found a wash tub full down in the spring house, all hardened and ready for use."

"That would be Rooster Wilson," Clara said. "He makes the most wonderful lye soap, but he doesn't ever put scent in it. He liked Myra and kept her supplied."

"Where'd the lavender come from?" Velvet asked.

"That was something Myra refused to be without. Her mother sent a year's worth of sweet lavender soap with her when she came out here from Louisiana." Joy said. "Lord, we thought we'd have to bury her parents when Hoyt wanted her to join him in Wyoming. He'd found this ranch, bought it for next to nothing because the man who had it found out right quick he didn't want a second winter in Wyoming, but Myra's mother couldn't imagine her baby girl outside the social life in the city."

"I see," Velvet nodded. "Well, ladies I found lots and lots of blooming rose blossoms, so today we are making hand milled rose soap, just like Lizzy used to make for us in South Carolina."

"Who's Lizzy?" Joy asked.

"Lizzy was a slave but she didn't belong to my grandparents. Grandfather was a preacher and the rich folks in the congregation loaned him their slaves to work for him. Lizzy was my surrogate mother and I loved her very much," Velvet said. "Here, Clara, you can pull the petals and get them ready for boiling. That's a sit-down job. Joy, you can begin to shave soap. Reckon that could be a sit-down job, too, until it begins to boil. Get ready ladies. In three weeks, everyone will think of spring when we walk through the doors."

"We had a slave like that," Joy said, picking up the sharp knife and carefully catching the shavings in a bowl. "What do you think is going to happen, Velvet? To the world we know. Momma and Daddy have slaves and there's a war brewing on the wind. Everyone is talking about it in the south."

"I think the South will eventually pull away from the northern states and we'll fight. I'm not so sure it's all about slaves. Both sides will suffer and neither will really come out winners because they'll both lose their men. The south is going to fight for their way of life to continue, though and it'll be a blood bath. Here, Clara, that's enough petals for the first boiling. We have to let them boil exactly three minutes then scoop them all out. Then the next batch goes in for three minutes and then the last. Three batches, three minutes each to make the rose water. That's the secret of good rose soap. Lots of petals but only three minutes, just long enough to draw out the oils. Now, where were we. Oh, the war. I have to tell you girls right up front. I'm not faulting no one for what they own or how they live, but I wouldn't ever own another human being. Lizzy and her daughter, Mandy, weren't some kind of animals to be owned. They were warm human beings with feelings and ideas."

"I grew up with a maid of my own," Clara said. "Never thought of the fact that Poppa owned her, but he did. Still owns a dozen or so. They live in the quarters out back of the big house and take care of the place for him. Poppa's a business man, not a farmer, so he doesn't need to own as many as some folks. You really think it will come to war?"

"Know it down in the bottom of my heart. Don't reckon ya'll will see as much of it out here in Wyoming as they'll see in South Carolina or even Virginia, but it's going to blow in on the wind before long," Velvet said.

"Well, we won't think of war today," Clara sighed. "We'll think of rose soap because war will mean something might happen to Cyrus and I couldn't bear that. Not a second time." She shuddered.

"Hey, do you know how to make this lye soap that I'm cutting all to pieces?" Joy said, glad to think about something other than politics. Her husband, Richard, talked war from daylight to dark. He was from Pennsylvania and grew up in a household with no slaves, of course. A deep south lady who'd been waited on since birth by black people, Joy didn't know how she felt about the whole issue. She just didn't want to think about Richard going to fight against her own brothers.

"Yes, I do. Want me to write it down for you so you can make it after I'm gone?" Velvet said. "Better yet, grab that pen and ink and a piece of paper from Hoyt's desk over there. Write while I talk and stir these petals. You already got enough shaved for the first go around of soap. I make small batches of milled soap. Seems to work better that way."

"Okay," Joy gathered the equipment, dipped the pen in ink and wrote, *Soap*, across the top. "I'm ready when you are."

"It's six and a half cups of tallow," Velvet began. "Good clean tallow, strained through a fine sieve. Seven eighths of a cup of lye. Two and a half cups of boiled, cooled water. You add the lye to the water, never the other way around. Make it outside if you can; if not then at least stir the lye into the water outside because it's some pretty powerful stuff. You need the ventilation or you'll drop in a dead faint. Lizzy always made several batches in one day but she made it all outside. We'd have had to bury Grandmother if that horrid smell got in her house." Velvet continued. "Now, you got that down? Next you get that water to just barely warm to your skin. Lizzy couldn't read or write so she just said make it a little bit warm to the fingertips. The tallow has to be melted to as near the exact same as the water and lye mixture. Then you slowly, slowly add the tallow to the water, in a fine stream. No bigger than Mandy's littlest finger, Lizzy said. Then the stirring begins. Stir and stir and stir, for at least an hour. Tracings will start to form on the surface just before it's ready to pour up in the molds. Wrap the molds in towels and set it up for two days. That was just perfect, because Lizzy only came every other day. So the second day, she'd test it. If it was ready— and it always was—she'd cut it into cakes. Then she'd put it on needlepoint canvas so it could breathe all the way around and set it down in the spring house to cure for three weeks. Usually after two weeks, though, she'd chose a day and we'd make rose soap for Grandmother. She hated plain soap and insisted on having her rose soap." Velvet smiled. "When I was sixteen she gave me my first cake of rose soap and I fell in love with it."

"Sounds easy, but I bet I mess up the first time," Joy laughed.

"Don't you go making lye soap until after that baby comes. Smelling that stuff might cause problems," Velvet shook her finger at Joy.

"Yes, ma'am," Joy said. "I'll surely wait. Besides if we make enough of this milled soap today, we won't need any more for a long time."

"That's right," Velvet said. "Now I think we're ready to add the soap and begin the stirring. Doesn't it smell heavenly in here?"

"It sure does," Clara smiled. Lord, but she'd like to keep Velvet forever. She'd never met a woman just like Velvet Dulan, and she was exactly what Hoyt needed, even if he was as stubborn as a Louisiana swamp rat and didn't know what was good for him.

"Now, the portions are a cup and a half of soap shavings to one cup plus a tablespoon of rose water. You add the shavings, Joy, a few at a time, and I'll stir."

"Doesn't seem so difficult, does it?" Joy said. "Here all this time, I thought there was some dark secret to making good scented soap. Wonder what other scents we could work with?"

"Well, if you can come by some chocolate powder and talk the infirmary out of some peppermint oil, you can make your beginning water from that and make a fine chocolate mint soap that men folk sometimes like to use. It's ugly as a mud fence but it's got a right nice odor. Or if you can mix a little clove oil and cinnamon sticks together, or clove oil and orange peel, it makes a right nice masculine soap," Velvet said. "Lizzy made Grandfather some kind of spicy smelling stuff, but I'm not sure about the portions."

"We could experiment," Joy said. "Next year when the lavender is—"

"No, I won't be here next year," Velvet said. "But you all can do it."

Clara pulled a few more petals from the roses. Next year

Velvet might not be here, but she wouldn't swear on that fact. Not after seeing that longing look in Hoyt's face when he looked up from kissing Velvet. No, she wouldn't make a bet on that fact at all.

At the end of the day, Hoyt stripped his filthy shirt, lowered his suspenders and washed his upper torso in the watering trough beside the barn. The sun set low on the horizon and his stomach grumbled. If he hadn't thought to take a couple of left-over breakfast biscuits and a hand full of those sugar cookies Velvet had made, he'd be starving by now. He'd miss her cooking when she left, that was true, however, given the choice, he'd cook his own supper and enjoy the solitude.

He opened the back door of the cabin, expecting a rush of lavender to fill his nose only to find the strong odor of roses combined with the yeasty aroma of baking bread. His mother used lavender soap; his grandmother had used it before her and Myra had loved it. So what was the rose odor?

"Bread will be finished in about ten minutes," Velvet said without looking up. "I made a pot of vegetable soup with a couple of jars of venison I put up last week. Some thick slices of bread should be good with it. Oh, I found a little cinnamon hiding back below the cook table so I made a few cinnamon rolls for dessert." She picked up the coffee pot and set it on the back of the stove to simmer and finally looked at Hoyt. She bit her tongue to keep from gasping. There he stood half naked. Soft black hair covered his chest and she suddenly longed to touch it. Could it possibly be as soft as it looked? His muscles were everywhere; on his upper arms, across his chest and stomach; his lower arms and even in his beefy looking shoulders. Doctors weren't supposed to look like that. They worked with their minds and hands; not their bodies.

Hoyt had been listening, but more than that, he'd been letting the mixed odors and the flush on Velvet's cheeks mesmerize him. She was truly beautiful since she'd regained her looks and strength. He could fall into those blue eyes and take a long, leisurely stroll through her heart and soul. When she smiled the world lit up all around her like a sunrise putting the moon to bed.

Finally, he realized she was staring at him and a slow heat crawled into his neck and cheeks. Lord, it had been years since anything or anyone had made Hoyt Baxter blush. "I'm sorry," he mumbled. "I washed up outside and should've at least thrown my shirt back on until I got into my room."

"Oh, nonsense," she said. "No need to put on a dirty shirt. Supper will be ready in five minutes." She turned quickly to check the bread even though she knew it wasn't ready. Anything to keep her eyes off that chest where she had the strangest urge to lay her face and listen to the beating of his heart. No, that would never, ever work. Hoyt Baxter would always be true to his sweet Myra's memory. He'd kissed Velvet a couple of times and turned her world upside down, but it was just a spur of the moment, a lonely man thing that amounted to nothing. Oh, but right then Velvet wished it could amount to something more.

"I was expecting the smell of lavender in the house," he said.

"No, we made rose soap today," she said. Something in her chest tightened. Hoyt preferred the sweet lavender to roses. Of course, he did. That was what Myra used and naturally he would always love it. She shouldn't even care what he liked, but the honesty in Velvet surfaced. In spite of her resolve not to like him, she did. Perhaps the age old theory had come to life: that which a person usually wants is what they most assuredly can not have.

She heard the bedroom door shut before she chanced

another glance in that direction. If she'd be able to continue the trip to California, would she have someday found herself liking the man she would have married there? As much as she was beginning to like the obstinate Dr. Baxter? She doubted it.

Hoyt opened the armoire door and gathered a hand full of his deceased wife's skirt tails to his nose. The lavender was there but it was faint. He had to shut his eyes tightly and use his imagination to conjure up the smell over the rose scent permeating everything in his cabin. Two scents: one of the past, the other of the very much alive present. He wanted to hang on to the lavender but the rose was so pleasant. It didn't completely replace the lavender but almost complimented it. He picked out a shirt and slipped his arms into it. It was the same shirt he'd worn the day he found Velvet in his bed when he came home from the cemetery. He recognized it by the mismatched button at the very bottom of the shirt tail. Yet, all the stains were gone and it was a brilliant white again. Velvet surely did know how to do a laundry. He'd give her that much credit.

He combed his black hair straight back and pulled his suspenders back up. He'd gotten entirely too comfortable around the woman. It was inexcusable for him to come into the house half naked before her. It would never happen again; he'd see to it. Velvet Dulan wasn't his type. No, not at all. She was too tall by at least five inches. He liked a small, petite woman with light hair and big brown eyes. Not a medium height lady with dark brown hair and clear blue eyes. No, not even if he did go looking, which he never would, he surely wouldn't choose someone like Velvet.

Velvet ladled out two bowls of soup, rich with potatoes, carrots, corn, green beans and shredded cabbage, along with the venison. She'd made it for lunch for Joy and Clara, along with a pan of cornbread, then sent home two quart jars each with them for their supper. It was impossible to make soup for two people. It made a huge pot full by the time everything got thrown in. Gotta-go soup, she remembered Lizzy calling it. "This has gotta go, and these leftover green beans from last night and this little bit of beef roast. All gotta go in the pot."

"Gotta go," Velvet said aloud. "Just like me. I gotta go even though my heart is dreading the day."

"I'm sorry. Were you talking to me?" Hoyt slung open the door and filled the room with his presence.

"No, to myself. Bread is almost done. Soup is cooling a bit while we wait," Velvet said, an edge to her voice that she couldn't control. Wasn't it just like her silly old heart to reject what it could have back in South Carolina when the elderly deacon offered to take her hand in marriage; then turn right about and want what it could not have here in Wyoming? Nothing made a bit of sense.

"Smells wonderful. I'm starving," he said, pulling up a chair and sniffing the steam from the top of the bowl. "We used to go visiting Momma's sister in Alabama and she had slaves. Seems like one of them made soup like this."

"Probably. Lizzy taught me to cook when I was a little girl. After she was gone I didn't go to the kitchen very often. The new cook scared the bejesus out of me. She was big as a barn door and never smiled. But when I left she was the only one who came to the stage station and told me good-bye," Velvet said, warmth creeping back into her tone.

It was more than she'd said in three days, and Hoyt attributed her good mood to feminine company. He'd have to tell her later that she could invite the girls anytime she wanted. He could easily disappear while they were there. "So you had slaves, too?"

"Oh, no!" She shook her head. She set the sliced bread

on the table between them, sat down at her place and bowed her head.

He gave a brief thanks. Blowing the soup gently before he put it into his mouth, he rolled his eyes in appreciation. It tasted even better than what he remembered his aunt's cook preparing for him and Boyd.

"We didn't have slaves. Grandfather is a preacher and the richer of the congregation loan him their slaves. One comes to cook every other day and another to do the yard work and another to clean the house. Lizzy was my favorite until the day I told my grandparents I wished I was her color and that she was my mother because she at least loved me."

The chuckle began in his chest as a low rumble then erupted into an all-out roar. He wiped his eyes with his napkin and got the hiccups. She watched in awe. The man could laugh at such a silly story. Or had he perhaps been sipping on a bottle of moonshine all day instead of doing whatever ranchers did out there on their land?

"Did you really say that? We didn't have slaves because Daddy's people were originally from the North and he forbid it, but I can just imagine what Momma would have done if I'd said something like that," he said.

"Well, Grandfather wasn't too happy. I got a whipping and had to pray on my knees for forgiveness for blasphemy for a whole hour. I didn't tell him I prayed that Lizzy and Mandy would someday be free to do what they pleased." She slathered her bread with sweet butter.

"So you think the North has a right to demand the South stop the slavery?" He asked.

"I had this discussion with the girls today," she said. "I don't think anyone has the right to own another human, no matter what color they are. But I don't think anyone has the right to tell them they can't either. It's a mixed-up feeling I have about it all. I hate to think of war, Hoyt, but it's coming sure as the moon will dawn tonight. The South has a genteel way of life, but it depends on slavery. They aren't going to stand aside and watch it blow away on the next breeze heading North just because the North is riding a high horse and making demands. Will you fight?"

"I don't know. I'm from a split family. My father is a lawyer in Louisiana. My mother came right off a southern plantation in Alabama and has no care whether she has slaves or not. My father pays a staff of people to work for her. I'm of the opinion that no one has the right to own another human, either. But to fight on the side of the North when they're making demands goes against my grain."

"So you might just stay here at the fort and take care of whoever comes in needing help?" She asked.

"I won't ever set foot in that fort again, nor will I doctor again. Southerners. Northerners. No one. I'll probably stay right here on this ranch and do what I do every day and let them fight their war," he said coldly.

She filled her mouth with soup and thought about what he'd said. Hoyt Baxter had too much passion to straddle the fence if war started. He'd be out there somewhere with his black bag taking care of the wounded and the ill. She'd be willing to bet all of her new rose soap on that issue. She'd be off in California or Nebraska by then and never know for sure, but he'd heal someday and when he did, he'd pick up those medical tools again. For right now, though, that war seemed far away and a lot less important that the one Velvet was battling inside her heart.

Chapter Ten

"I'm going to the cemetery," Hoyt said on Sunday morning as he laid his Bible to the side.

"I'm going to church," Velvet said.

"Surely not!" He raised an eyebrow. "Didn't Opal tell you to stay out of there? Don't you know she's the general's wife? Talk used to have it that he didn't make a decision of any magnitude without consulting her first. Officers sometimes call it Fort Opal behind his back."

"Yes, Opal said for me to stay away. I've been praying about that. Spent a long time on my knees, and God hasn't told me not to go. I think He carries even more weight than dear old Opal," Velvet said.

What Hoyt would have given to see what Opal would do when she walked into the Chapel and found Velvet there couldn't be measured in bushels and pecks. No one, to his knowledge, had ever stood up against Opal. The fact that Clara didn't go back to the fort with her a few days ago was pretty brave, but for Velvet to walk into that chapel, right on the fort, after she'd been told publicly to stay away—why that took sheer nerve. He'd have to watch the sky to see if there was an explosion on the fort in the middle of the morning. It would probably rain parts of Opal's violent fury for weeks. Hoyt sure didn't envy the general, having to live with her. It might be the perfect time for him to choose a hundred men and go outside the fort on maneuvers.

"Well, you been warned," Hoyt said, slipping his feet into boots. "Take the buggy with you. You might need a quick get-away."

Holy smoke! Would wonders never cease? Hoyt had actually smiled and made a joke. Could it be that he was afraid of Opal? No. Surely not. Hoyt wasn't afraid of anything—except his own heart.

"Thank you. I will do just that. But don't worry about me, Hoyt. I can take care of myself," she assured him as started up to the loft. She could wear her nice Sunday shoes if she didn't have to walk. Careful not to bump her head again, she fetched them from under the bed, and put them on, fastening all the little buttons up the sides.

She left at the same time she had the week before, but it didn't take as long to get to the fort in a horse-drawn buggy. She'd been surprised to find it all ready when she got to the barn, but Hoyt was no where to be seen for her to thank. It seemed like since the cemetery event, they'd come to a new understanding one where he wasn't constantly on guard. It was a bit like a couple of children who'd found themselves living next door to each other. Like a boy and a girl, both of whom didn't like the opposite sex but still would like to have someone to talk to and play with in the long afternoons. So they laid aside their differences and became wary friends at first. That's where they were, she decided as she slipped the reins from between her gloved fingers in front of the chapel. Something more than mere acquaintances, more like wary friends, waiting to see what the next move would be; not surprised at a show of temper but hoping there might come a time when she'd play soldiers with him, and he'd have a tea party with her. Disregarding those two smoldering kisses, that was. No little boy and girl could have ever exchanged kisses like that.

"We won't ever be true friends," she assured herself as she parked the buggy.

The guard didn't try to hide his grin when she had stated her business that morning. Either he thought she was out of her mind, or else he was waiting for her to tell him that she was setting up business down on the banks of the river in tar-paper shanty.

No one was in the chapel so she slid across the back pew to the end; the very same place she'd sat the week before. "No," she said aloud. "I'm not slinking around and fearing Opal or her wrath." She marched right up to the front pew and sat down next to the center aisle, let her Bible fall open where it would and read a passage in Psalms 66.

"Make a joyful noise unto God . . . sing forth the honor of his name . . . through the greatness of Thy power shall Thy enemies submit themselves unto thee," she read. She looked up at the empty pulpit, trying to make sense of the words. Would she have the power to bend Opal? She doubted that. Even God might have trouble doing that. But she could make a joyful noise. There sat a piano and no one had played last week. Surely one of the ladies could play but perhaps Opal had decreed they would sing without accompaniment.

The sound of her heels on the wooden floor made a tapping noise as she went forward, to the left side of the church and pulled out the piano bench. Inside the bench, she found several hymnals. She chose the one she'd used in South Carolina when she played for services in the United Methodist Church where her grandfather preached every week. She stretched her fingers and set the book on the piano. She'd make a joyful noise all right. They might run her joyful noise right out of the place, but she would do what God told her.

She began to play, first one song then the next one. By the time she was on page twelve people had began to come inside. The preacher first, whose face beamed with a smile. He sat down on the deacon's bench behind the pulpit and opened his Bible, reading as he listened. Clara, Joy and a handful of other women took their places on the second pew. Clara waved at her; Joy smiled.

The church was full when Opal's robust frame filled the doorway, blocking the light. Little jerky movements made her head look like it was going to fall off and roll down the aisle, until she found the person responsible for playing the piano without her consent. Velvet caught her eye and smiled sweetly.

It was the smile that threw Opal into a tantrum. She marched straight to the pulpit and held up her hand for Velvet to stop playing. *In for a lamb, in for a sheep*, Velvet thought, and played to the end of the hymn before she stopped, laid her hands in her lap and got ready for whatever sermon with which Opal intended to send them all to hell.

The chaplain cleared his throat and started toward the podium. Opal might be the general's wife, but she was just another woman inside the walls of his chapel. At least that's what he thought until she turned her wrath-filled eyes on him. She pointed back toward the deacon's bench and said, "You sit down! I'll have my say before these services begin, and you'll sit right there or the general will send you somewhere where you'll be dead in twenty four hours."

The chaplain sat down.

"I will not have this woman in my church. I don't care if she plays the piano and if she's got some of you thinking she's a saint with a golden halo. She's a harlot living out there with that murderer, and she's not welcome here. I proved it myself. Went out there to give them a benefit of a doubt and found them in bed together. You are not fit for decent folks to share a church with. So leave," Opal pointed her finger at the back door and glared at Velvet.

A while back, Velvet would have tried to hide under the piano keys, but that was before she'd met the other Dulan sisters, who had assured her that the day would come when she'd have a backbone made of iron like theirs. She stood straight and tall and walked right up beside Opal whose face was scarlet and eyes were no more than slits in a face of wrinkles and sagging skin.

"I told you last week that when God told me I couldn't come in here, then I'd listen to him. I prayed real hard this week about coming back to church. God didn't tell me I couldn't come back so here I am. Did you pray about your sins, Opal? Did you ask Him to forgive you for judging without knowing and for telling lies? Did you really find us in bed together? You want to tell this congregation the real story? I don't intend to tell them anything. But you can if you want to. And you can leave if my presence bothers you. You and all the rest of the people in this church, but I'm not leaving. I'm staying right here until services are over and if the preacher doesn't mind, I think I'll play the piano, too. I played for the United Methodist Church for years in South Carolina. I miss that part of my service to God."

"My word is law in this fort!" Opal shouted. "Get out!"

"God's word is law in His church, whether it's Methodist, Baptist, Lutheran, Catholic or whatever. We founded this nation on the principal that we have the freedom of worship. You ever read the Constitution, ma'am." Velvet said.

Opal drew back her hand and was on her way to slap Velvet's face when a vice grip stopped it mid-air. "I think that's enough out of you," the chaplain said quietly. "If you can't sit down over there in your pew, then you better go on home."

"I'll go home and I'll have the general back here in five minutes to clean out this hornet's nest," she declared vehemently.

"You do that," the chaplain said. "Now if you'll all open your hymnals to song number 89, we'll sing. Miss Velvet, if you'd be so kind as to play for us?" He nodded toward the piano.

Velvet took her place, utterly dumfounded that her heart wasn't beating triple time. She played the first chords and the audience began to sing, loudly and with more robust than they'd sang last week. Two songs later, the chaplain asked everyone to bow for a moment of silent prayer in which they should remember their private battles and needs. Velvet prayed earnestly for Hoyt Baxter to find peace someday. She heard Lizzy's admonition from when she was a small girl while her eyes were shut. It was a hot summer South Carolina day and the lady who owned Lizzy had come to tea at the manse, bringing her daughter along to play with Velvet. Grandmother had told Velvet to play with the child in the rose garden. Once there the little girl had told Velvet that they would play house and Velvet would be the slave or she'd take back the dress Velvet was wearing since her mother had given it to the church to be given to the poor and needy. Velvet had been livid when she told Lizzy about it, and Lizzy told her to pray for the little girl.

"Pray for her! I want to shoot her dead," Velvet stamped her foot.

"You pray for her. She's a willful child and she needs your prayers."

The conversation came back in a flash in the silence of the church, and Velvet didn't need a written decree to know what it meant. She prayed for Opal right then, asking God to forgive her for her black heart, and if she couldn't or wouldn't change, then would he please heap a few coals of fire upon her head. When she raised her head, the chaplain cleared his throat, opened his Bible and made a few opening remarks. Before he could even begin the sermon the back doors swung open and the general himself surveyed the whole congregation. A few enlisted men slunk down in their seats, hoping he didn't see them. Clara and Joy both stiffened their backs and silently dared him to send their men off to something wilder than Wyoming.

The general stepped aside and Opal, with a red face and swollen eyes to match, was right behind him. "Do continue, good man," the general said in a soft voice. "We're sorry we are a bit late, but we had a couple of things to straighten out before we could attend service this morning. I heard the beautiful music through the open windows of my study. I'm so glad we've a lady who can play now. We'll just take our seat and listen to the sermon."

A hush fell over the congregation and the chaplain ran a finger around his collar. So the general had finally reached his fill of hen-pecking. That should be good morale for everyone at the fort. However, the chaplain had chosen to preach on submission this morning and for the life of him, not another passage came to mind. *Lord, please, give me some words that I can say. It's the first time in a year that the general has attended services. Please give me something neutral*, he prayed silently as he looked down at the hymnal. A song. That's what he'd do. Sing a song and something would come to him.

"Well, since you missed the first hymns, maybe if Miss Velvet wouldn't mind, we'll just sing another one before my message," he said.

The general nodded with a smile. Opal kept her eyes on the hymnal in her lap.

They sang.

The preacher waited for something to come to him.

God said no.

He preached on submission: to the Father in heaven; wives to their husbands; enlisted men to their superiors. He wondered the whole time if it would be his last sermon at Fort Laramie.

After the benediction, given by the general, the people filed silently out to the court yard. Opal stood stoically beside her husband when he shook Velvet's hand and told her again how much he enjoyed the music. Opal ignored her.

"In South Carolina, Sunday afternoons are for visiting," Velvet said to the women, standing in two groups, one slightly behind Opal, the others loosely beside their husbands and Clara. "I will be at home at Dr. Hoyt Baxter's cabin this afternoon for those of you interested in tea and cookies. I can not vouch for the doctor. He often has duties he takes care of on Sunday afternoons at the cemetery where his wife, son and brother are laid to rest. He may or may not be there, but I will and I would enjoy the company of any of you ladies who would be kind enough to come visiting. Anytime between one and two would be nice. Good day, sir," she said to the general.

"You'll be sitting there all alone eating your cookies and drinking your tea," Opal said.

"That's enough. Didn't you listen to what the good man said in there?" the general said. "Good day to you, Miss Velvet."

One of the enlisted men handed her up into the buggy seat and she drove out of the fort, wondering the whole time if she would indeed spend the afternoon alone. If she didn't, would there be a huge fight with Hoyt over her impetuosity in inviting all of the ladies to the ranch without even asking him? His Sunday afternoon would be ruined and he'd be madder than a hungry wolf with its foot in a trap.

Chapter Eleven

Hoyt sat down in front of the three graves. He pictured Myra's pretty face that last day before she went into labor with the baby, then the blue face of his son who refused to breathe, and then his brother in those last minutes when the fever raged in his body and there was nothing Hoyt could do. A soft, gentle wind stirred the leaves in the trees and Hoyt looked up, letting the air dry the tears on his face.

"Lord, I'm so confused," he whispered.

He sat there for more than an hour before he finally stood up and started back toward the house. He walked slowly, wishing he could go back to the spring before and redo everything, but that miracle wasn't his to have. When he rounded the last curve before the cabin, he looked up to see two buggies parked beside the porch. Two men lounged on the front porch swing and he could hear the chatter of women floating on the wind.

"What is going on here?" He asked as he threw the horse reins over the hitching rail and stepped up on his own porch.

"Hello, Dr. Baxter," Cyrus stood and extended his hand. "You'll remember Richard Callaway?"

"Yes, hello to you both," Hoyt said. "But what are you doing at my house?"

"Well, Velvet kind of turned the fort around this morning in church. Reckon us men might go out toward the barn. The Women folk are having a Sunday afternoon tea and cookies. We just drove the buggies out here for them. Wouldn't think of intruding on their time. Kind of like in the South when they used to go out in the gardens and we'd take our cigars to the library. Let's pretend we're taking some cigars to the library, Dr. Baxter," Cyrus said.

Hoyt nodded in agreement. Velvet's laughter sifted out from the others and he could tell she was having a wonderful time. That was all well and good, except no one bothered to ask for his ideas on Sunday afternoon visits. and Cyrus was also the one who'd taken his brother's place in Clara's heart, so he wasn't so sure how he felt about spending an afternoon with him, either. Velvet sure had a way of stirring up pots of problems, and he'd be the first one to tell her about it when this party was finished. One thing for sure, it would be the last one on his ranch. He'd see to that. He valued his self-imposed solitude, and no one was taking it from him.

"This is a big thing for the women, Dr. Baxter," Richard said. "They're cooped up in the fort nearly all the time. To come out here where it's almost like being at home, well, it's a real treat. That Velvet Dulan is a jewel. I hope she has Sunday afternoon teas often. Joy sure had a good time at the soap making the other day, too. I guess I'm rattling on, sir, when Cyrus wants to tell you about this morning."

"Cyrus?" Hoyt accepted the cigar from him, lit it and waited.

"Seems like Velvet has done wrestled the fort away from Opal and given it back to the general. He's walking pretty tall, and I don't know which one will be the worst to follow, but at least it's back where it's supposed to be," Cyrus said. "I hope Velvet winters here with you, Hoyt. She's a breath of fresh air to us all. Taking care of that Indian problem and now the Opal problem, too." He proceeded to tell the tale of what happened in church that morning.

Sunday afternoon teas to continue? Velvet wintering with him? It might happen the day that the Devil and the angels danced a jig together, but not on his ranch in Wyoming. Hoyt did listen to the Cyrus' story though, and couldn't contain the chuckle when Cyrus repeated word for word what Velvet said to Opal about God not telling her to stay out of the church. That girl sure had some nerve or was more stupid than a box of rocks. "What happened when it was over?" he asked.

"Velvet waltzed out the door and said she was settin' up a Sunday tea like they have in the South. Where folks visit and have at-homes. This week she said she would be at home. I reckon one of the other wives will be at home next week. Some of the teas will have to be inside the fort because that's where we live. You and Myra never had to live in it, but we do if we aren't thinking about staying in this part of the world and don't have the money to buy a place of our own. Anyway, this is all very good for the women," Cyrus said.

"And Opal?" Hoyt asked, remembering well the look on the woman's face when she caught him kissing Velvet.

"Well," Richard rubbed his chin. "She would've liked to show her fangs but the general put her in her place. Never saw anything like it in the two years I've been here. I don't reckon she'll be having any at-homes or going to them either."

"Me neither," Hoyt said, honestly. Was this his answer? Did God look down on his pitiful plea out there and send him company?

"Heard you was culling out the cattle and going to send some with the drive coming through," Richard said. "We got word Friday they would be here by the end of the week. Just a scout who'd been out and seen them, but that might give you a little more of a time table to get things ready."

"Thank you," Hoyt said.

"And Doc, if you want to come back to the fort as a civilian, I bet the general would sure hire you," Cyrus said.

"No thank you," Hoyt shook his head. "I'm just a common old rancher now. I've quit the doctoring business for good."

"No harm in asking," Cyrus nodded. "Been a while since I had to sit in the library while the ladies had their social. What you got in there?" He looked at the barn doors.

"Couple of work horses, a sorry old stubborn mule, an almighty fine riding horse, a buggy and a litter of kittens," Hoyt said honestly, not realizing until that moment how much he'd missed the camaraderie of other men.

"Reckon we might look at the kittens. Lord, it's been a hundred years since I held a baby kitten in my hands," Cyrus asked, his brown eyes dancing with excitement. "Don't you go tellin' Velvet I'm a sucker for baby kittens neither. She'll tell Clara and that'll blow my tough soldier act all to smitheeens."

"Wouldn't dream of it," Hoyt said, leading the way into the domain of men. The barn, where they could talk about tack, horses, soldering and fields, and whether to take a big chance and plant in April or wait for sure until the last frost had fought its last battle before spring was really born.

Velvet sat in one rocker and Clara in the other. Four other women had seats around the table. She'd set the coffee pot in the middle of the table and piled the cookies high on a platter at exactly one o'clock. No one would come, she'd convinced herself by one thirty when she reheated the coffee. At one forty, two buggies drove up in the yard and five women marched up to the front door.

She'd never been so happy in all her life when she opened the door and bid them good afternoon. There wasn't a silver tray sitting on a credenza inside the door to take their cards; there were no cards. But it was as close as she could get to a genteel Sunday afternoon.

"And do you think Fort Laramie will still be in operation when the war does break out?" Joy asked. "What will that do to us women? Will they send us home to be right in the middle of the fighting or let us stay here with our men folks?"

Velvet had been gathering wool and wasn't sure how the conversation got on war again. Seemed that was all anyone talked about these days. It must be a military thing. She never once heard it mentioned when she was traveling on the wagon train. More than a hundred women and one little girl named Merry Briley and not a word of war. Of course, they were all going to face something worse than a war. Hank had told them when they reached Bryte, California, he'd put all their names in a hat. The men who'd paid for the brides would each draw a name. No one had a say-so about who they married. If there weren't battles waged, fights won and lost, and a whole war in each and every one of those households during the year after the multiple weddings that day, Velvet would walk all the way back to South Carolina and marry that elderly deacon her grandfather chose for her.

"What do you think, Velvet?" Joy asked.

"I'm so sorry. I was gathering wool," she admitted.

"So what do you think about it?" Clara repeated.

"About what? War? I wouldn't know what they'll decide. The government will write a million pages concerning it, I'm sure, and Opal might even help," Velvet tried to make light of the situation.

"So, what were you thinking about?" Clara asked. "Hoyt?"

Silence filled the room. A feather hitting the floor right then would have sounded like a blast from a cannon.

"No, actually, I wasn't." Velvet smiled. "I was thinking about all those women on that train I had to leave. You know they are going to marry a man without even knowing him. Each man gets to pick a name from a hat and fate takes care of all of it."

"Good grief," Joy said.

"Good a way as any," Stella laughed. "How many of us really know a man until we live with him anyway? What you bet the ones who're out there on the porch are wondering what we're saying about them right now? Their egos are bigger than their hats."

"Not my Cyrus," Clara threw up her hands in mock despair. "Surely not my precious Cyrus. Why, the first thing out of his mouth will be 'And my pretty darling, did you ladies discuss politics?' and the second will be 'What did they say about me and Richard?' Men folks think women live only to think about them and keeping their pride filled to capacity. That's why we love them. They think we're stupid and we know they are."

"Clara!" Velvet gasped.

"It's the truth," Joy said with a giggle. "We love them enough to over look it is all. Now you going to tell us about living out here with Hoyt or not? Is he still an old bear?"

"You got that right," Velvet said. "With an ingrown toenail, a sore tooth and a growling stomach. But as soon as a wagon train comes through, I'll leave him and be gone. Either way. To California to live with my sister, Gussie, or to Nebraska to live with my sister, Willow. Doesn't really matter to me. Just so long as I'm gone. He'll dance a jig in the pig trough the day I leave so if you girls want to see a sight, then make a trip out here and watch the show."

"Okay, ladies, we both got duty tonight and we'd like a nap," Cyrus called from the front door.

"It's been wonderful," Stella said for all of them. "Next week, I'll be at home if any of you ladies would like to pay a visit. As you all know the Lieutenant and I live just outside the fort in a little house. The children will be there under our feet but that's the way of things. Before long Clara will have to bring along her baby. I'm so glad we've started these socials. Good day, Velvet. Oh, hello, Dr. Baxter. So good to see you again. You might bring Velvet to the at-home next Sunday, sir."

"We'll see about that," Hoyt said. "Cattle drive is coming through. I might be busy, but she's quite capable of driving herself."

"Yes, I guess she is," Stella said with a wink.

Velvet sat on the porch swing and waved until there was nothing but a dust cloud and it was dissipating quickly. Hoyt hadn't shouted or even given her a mean look so apparently he wasn't too upset about her invading his privacy with a bunch of women folk.

"So what did you talk about in there?" He asked.

She bit her tongue but could no more answer with giggling than she could have risen to Heaven and visited with Jake Dulan for an hour.

"You going to answer me?" He asked, this time a cutting edge to his voice. He'd enjoyed the afternoon with Cyrus and Richard, but she really had no right opening his and Myra's home to a bunch of cackling old hens.

"Of course," Velvet said when she finally got her thoughts under control. "We discussed the war that's coming. We wondered what the government would do with Fort Laramie and whether the women and children would be sent home or if they could stay."

"Sure you did," Hoyt said. "Women don't discuss politics. They haven't a mind that deals with that kind of thing."

"And just what makes you an authority on what women talk about?" Velvet said coldly. How dare him underestimate a woman's brain! They were as capable as men, maybe even more so.

"I'm not stupid." He glared at her. What had happened to the wonderful afternoon? *C'est la guerre*, he thought, remembering the Louisiana dialogue he'd not thought of in a long time. This is war and it was indeed. A war of minds, of wills and of hearts. Velvet Dulan didn't know anything about war or politics and that was a fact.

"Neither am I, Hoyt Baxter," she said, glaring right back at him.

"Then why are you being so evasive?"

"I'm not. What did you big strong men talk about out there in the barn? I saw you tie up the horse and heard Cyrus say you should go to the library to smoke your cigars to give us some privacy. It was a nice gesture. So what did you talk about? I'm sure you talked about the newest fashion in lady's hats?" She turned the tables around on him.

"We talked about horses, cattle drives and planting. We even talked about baby kittens," he said defensively.

"Sure you did. Everyone knows men aren't real partial to baby kittens," Velvet said, flouncing into the house.

"What did they say about me?" Hoyt raised his voice an octave. "That I was a crazy old hermit?"

Velvet stopped in her tracks. "What did the men say about me? That I was a crazy old harlot?" She shot right back.

"I'd kill a man who said that about you," he said without thinking. Lord, what would she do with that comment? Think she could live here forever?

"Well, that's a nice thought on Sunday afternoon, Hoyt," she said. "I'm going to take a nap."

"Did they say that about me?" He was in the door and blocking her way up the stairs.

"No, they didn't. Strange as it may seem, and I do hate to deflate your ego, but we don't spend all our time talking about our men folk," she said, pushing her way past him and fighting the tingles in her bare arm where it had brushed against his. Lord Almighty, what would he think of that comment? That she considered him hers?

"Have a good rest, Velvet," he said with no trace of coldness in his voice. "Me, I think I'll stretch out for a long afternoon nap, too."

"Same to you, Dr. Baxter," she said, hoping to wipe that silly grin off his face.

It didn't work.

Chapter Twelve

Hoyt loved Wyoming but lately his thoughts went more and more to Louisiana, to his childhood home near Baton Rouge. When he'd buried Myra and the baby, then Boyd, he'd declared that he'd stay right there in Wyoming, never leaving them. Since Velvet came into his life though, things had changed. Like she said, war was coming. It might be five years; it might be next year, but the southern states and their sisters to the north were sure enough firing the first warning rounds with all their arguing.

He tried to sort through the foreign idea of leaving Wyoming as he rode up to the old line shack at the farthest western corner of his land and corralled all the cattle he planned to sell that morning. Cyrus had said the drive would probably be coming through Friday which was to-day, and the easiest way for the drive boss to see what he had up for sale was to pen them. One hundred head of mixed-breed cattle milled about inside the two crowded pens, bawling to be let back out into the wide open spaces.

Would that be what he did if he went back to city life? Would he feel cooped up and yearn for Wyoming's wide open spaces again? His mother and father, along with his younger two sisters and brother, would be elated to have him come home. But what would he do once he got there? His training was in the medical field and he'd forsaken that. Other than medicine, all he knew was soldiering, and that didn't appeal to him anymore since Boyd wasn't around to share it. That and ranching, which had been his salvation when the tragedies occurred last year. The old fellow who sold him the ranch had left the cattle and most of the furniture. At the time, it was an absolute blessing. Now he wondered—if he hadn't been tied to the ranch where would he be today?

Looking back, he had merely followed Boyd into the military, not wanting his brother to go off to all those adventures without him. It had been so easy back then. Boyd, out of college with a lawyer's degree; Hoyt, fresh out of medical school. All branches of the military were begging for doctors and they sure weren't turning lawyers away either, so both of them enlisted. What was just going to be an adventure for a few years had turned into a nightmare forever.

He leaned across the saddle horn and roughly counted the cows one more time. Maybe he'd add five more to the herd, or if he was serious about going back south, he should sell them all while he had the chance. He rode out and gathered in ten more rangy steers, edging them toward the corrals. He'd barely shut the gate when one steer threw back his head and bawled, rolling his eyes and charging into the fence. Hoyt jumped back in time to avoid the long horns slipping through the wooden planks.

The dust boiling up around the pens made him sneeze several times. Grit filled his eyes even with the bandanna up around his nose. He'd call it a day. A good day, at that. Although he hadn't decided one thing about where to spend the rest of his life, he'd gotten the cattle ready for market.

He kneed his horse gently and they started back toward

the cabin. He hoped Velvet had some more of those sugar cookies on the table when he arrived. One moment Hoyt was whistling; the next he was flying through the air like a rag doll. A dusting of fine sand which covered a slab of rock flew up and into his eyes when the back of his head slammed against it. The last thing Hoyt remembered before everything went dark was that he didn't want to die.

Velvet sneezed and flour flew up from the table and stuck in her eyes. She fumbled her way to the pump and blindly filled the dishpan with cold water and flushed her eyes. Flour was just a finely ground wheat, so why did it sting so badly? Just that little bit had soaked every bit of the moisture from her eyeballs and now they felt like they had gravel glued to them. She flushed them some more and sneezed again, spraying water from the pan all over the front of her dress.

She gave thanks that the bread itself was in the pans for the last raising, covered with a clean white dish towel, and all that she'd sneezed on was the table full of flour where she'd been kneading. Surely, she wasn't coming down with a summer fever. No, she assured herself, it was just a snoot full of flour and a simple sneeze.

Hoyt didn't come home for lunch so she had a jelly sandwich and a cup of coffee and went outside to work on the flower beds. Somehow in the course of the week, she'd never gotten around to taking care of them. She pulled weeds, dead-headed out enough marigolds to make half a cup of seeds, broad casted them on the other side of the house for the next year's crop, and then attacked the rose bushes. It was too early to give them a good pruning but she snipped hips and cut back the dead limbs. By the middle of the afternoon, she was dirty, sweaty and hot, so she dragged the bath tub in from the hook on the back porch and filled it. First with the hot water in the stove reservoir and then with several buckets of cold water from the pump.

Barefoot and about to be naked as soon as she came out of her camisole, corset and drawers, she remembered the rose soap. It wouldn't have had nearly enough time to set up proper, but if she took a spoon to dip it with and a towel to carry it in, it might have enough form she could at least have a bath with it. She looked every which way at the back door. Hoyt never had come home in the middle of the afternoon. Either he came for a half an hour to an hour at lunch and was gone again, or else he didn't arrive until supper time. But she'd feel like an awful fool getting caught, running out to the spring house in her under garments. No one was about, so she sprinted barefoot with a towel in her hands to the spring house. She'd just gotten a big, heaping spoon full of semi-hardened rose soap in her towel, when she stepped on a slug in her bare feet.

She danced a jig on her heels, trying to .shake the abominable creature from her between her toes, but it didn't work. She didn't dare throw the towel down or her soap would be lost and she couldn't get the stinky mess off her foot. She walked gingerly all the way back to the house on her heel and wondered the whole way why on earth Noah would have wanted to save two of those miserable things.

Once inside, she laid her towel wrapped treasure on the table, grabbed a mop rag and commenced to scrubbing the dead, slimy thing from her foot. She swore she'd throw the rag in the brush fire and never use it again, not even to mop the porches with. It would never be put in her laundry water. Her nose snarled and twitched when she imagined reaching into the tub and grabbing a rag with the wet remains of a slug on it.

Finally, when she was satisfied there wasn't even one shiny streak left between under her toes, she eased herself down into the bath water. The soap wasn't hardened yet, but by lathering up what she had in the wash cloth, she was able to use it quite effectively to wash her whole body. She laid back, enjoying the simple pleasure of being wet, and heard a distant clap of thunder. Hoyt would probably come home early for supper if it began to rain, she thought as she laid her head back on the edge of the tub and fell asleep.

The water was stone cold when a big clap of thunder awoke her. She jumped out of the tub, dried herself hurriedly and dressed in her yellow calico dress. Faded though it was, it still served its purpose and Hoyt never noticed whether she was dressed up or not. She scolded herself in mumbles for even thinking or caring what Hoyt liked or didn't like.

Dark clouds produced thunder and lightening but Hoyt still didn't come home. She'd made beans that morning and planned to fry a skillet of potatoes seasoned with onions, but it was senseless to begin that part of supper before he got there. Wrapping her arms around her waist, she stepped out on the back porch and looked off to the west which was the way he usually came from. No Hoyt. Maybe he'd gotten caught in the storm and had to hole up until it passed. Well, that served him right. A man, especially a doctor, should be able to look up at the sky and see the black clouds and surely he could hear the thunder.

She grabbed her work boots from inside the back door and crammed her bare feet into them. The odor of rain was everywhere and the clouds had obliterated the sun, but still nothing fell on her as she ran to the barn to see if maybe he was inside taking care of his horse before he came to the house. She found the horse, still saddled with its head hanging low, holding its swollen leg up, standing next to its stall.

Hoyt was out there somewhere without a horse and in this weather. Maybe hurt. Probably furious. She'd have to go find him. He'd said something this morning about gathering cattle for the drive coming through their part of Wyoming. She took time to unsaddle the horse, lead him to a stall, rub him down half way at least and toss a few fork fulls of hay over the top of the gate. Then she hitched up the work wagon with one horse, and climbed into the rough wood seat. It reminded her of driving when she was with the wagon train; only this was a lot smaller scale.

She followed the ruts to the west, hoping the whole time that she'd find Hoyt cussing mad and walking toward the house. Lightening flashed through the darkness, splitting one tree in half and setting it on fire, then the rain started. Drops as big as silver dollars fell and she could hear them sizzle as they hit the flaming tree.

Still no Hoyt.

She wiped her the water from her eyes and wished she'd taken time to at least put her hair back up before she rushed off into the storm hunting for a man who would be angry when she did find him. He'd mentioned something about corralling the cattle near the old line shack. If she found him in there, dry as bone and waiting out the storm, she intended to give him the sharp side of her tongue and perhaps the back side of her hand to boot.

She kept going on in spite of the driving wind that brought the cold rain in sheets to beat against her already dripping wet clothing. The trail played out at a crossroads. She sat there, bewildered, wet and fighting a temper fit. Did she go left or right? Suddenly, she heard a cow bawl in the distance. She sat very still, her long, limp wet hair hanging in her face, and listened. Nothing. She shut her eyes so she could concentrate on sounds and heard the faint cow's cry again. It might be a heifer who'd lost her baby in the storm and was crying for it, or hopefully it was the cows Hoyt had penned up for the sale. At least it gave her a reason to go right. She snapped the reins against the horse's flanks and he reluctantly turned right.

The form of the line shack appeared as an apparition through the rain. Cows were penned up in three separate corrals, all of them facing the southwest; a few of them protesting their quarters. She jumped down from the wagon seat and ran toward the shack. "Hoyt, I'm going to strangle you," she screamed as she kicked the door open. The hollow sound of an empty cabin greeted her. She wanted nothing more than to sit down and bawl like the cows, but she had to find him, even if it did mean going right back out. Shielding her eyes with the back of her hand, she took two steps toward the wagon when she saw something white lying out there not far from the last corral. It looked like a man's shirt. She took off at a dead run, the fierce wind trying to beat her back into the shack.

She dropped down on her knees when she realized it really was Hoyt and he wasn't moving. He lay flat on his back, his eyes closed. Rain, mixing with blood from a wound on the back of his head, ran in rivulets, puddling up under his back. She laid her head on his chest and listened so intently her ears hurt. There was a good, strong heart beat so he was just knocked out.

Hopefully.

She hoped nothing was broken as she raised his head and looped her arms under his, dragging his dead weight by inches back toward the shack. After three feet, her boots gave way and she slipped, dropping him like a sack of potatoes and falling across his chest. Salty tears and clean rain water combined as she made herself get back up and try again. She'd make it a foot or two, stop to huff and puff and then go again. Her arms were nothing more than limp noodles by the time she reached the open door of the old shack, but she'd made it.

A high pitched giggle escaped from her mouth and she

wondered where it came from. There wasn't one funny thing in the whole incident. "Drat it, Hoyt, wake up!" She screamed so loud the lone, dirty window pane trembled. With the last of strength she pulled him inside the twelve foot square room and slammed the door shut. She laid beside him, panting for several minutes, before she could catch her second wind.

He was as still as death and other than a beating heart, he might have well been nothing but a corpse. Tears continued to stream down her cheek bones. She'd never told him that she liked him and he was probably going to die. Liked him, nothing, she loved the man and there wasn't a thing she could do about it now. Wasn't that just like her Dulan luck? Always a day late for everything.

She looked at the bloody line coming from the doorway to where they both lay. She sat up and using every bit of her renewed energy, rolled him over on his side. The gash on the back of his head was deep and nasty looking. Probably had dirt and who knew what else in there already setting up infection. She needed supplies and all the doctoring things were back at the house. She'd simply have to go get them, she told herself, dreading that unavoidable ride back in the chilly rain.

She kissed his forehead and was going out the door when a mouse ran across the floor and up the wall, through a hole in the corner of the ceiling. She jumped back and knocked a chair into a cabinet situated behind the door. Glass rattled and a bottle rolled across the floor, coming to rest at her feet. Whiskey. It was a half a bottle of pure golden whiskey. The best thing in the world to wash out a wound.

She picked it up and began to search. Evidently Hoyt had spent some time last winter here, and she might find what she needed without making that trip back to the cabin. In a box under the edge of the cot she found a small sewing box with needles and thread, a dozen or so candles, and a box of matches. In another box there were jars of beans, tomatoes and corn and a tin of flour. The cabinet behind the door held a frying pan and a black iron kettle.

Wincing for him, she shuddered when she poured the whiskey in the gaping wound right under the hair line, running from just under his left ear about three inches across the back of his head. He moaned, but he didn't open his eyes, and for that she was thankful. It was going to hurt like the very devil and she wasn't as good as her younger sister, Willow, when it came to sewing up skin.

When she ran the needle through the fire, she noticed that her hands and fingernails were filthy. She couldn't take a chance of dirt falling into the gash. "Well there is plenty of water coming down outside," she said in a nervous voice that sounded foreign even to her own ears. She laid the needle down and opened the door. The rain seemed even colder than when it first began. Fall must be on the way. Gasping when the cold water hit her face, she held her hands straight out, rubbing them together to clean them. She'd pour the rest of the whiskey over them when she went inside. That was the best she could do.

Carefully, she tossed her hair down her back and went back to do a job she thoroughly hated. She reheated the needle until it was scarlet on the tip and hoped that killed any deadly things it might have on it, unwrapped fifty feet of thread from the spool until she was satisfied that whatever might have been exposed to grime would be gone. She hated to put the pressure on the needle to poke it through his skin, but there wasn't any other choice. She positioned the needle and shut her eyes, pushing until she had to open them to see what to do next. Small stitches. Close together. And leave off the last one in case infection set in so it would have a place to drain. Each one should have been easier than the last, but it wasn't. Every one brought a new batch of frustrated tears flowing down her cheeks.

"If you don't live, I won't go to your sorry old funeral," she threatened. "Making me do a job I hate. You better not die on me, Hoyt Baxter, not before I've had time to tell you my mind. Willow was willing to ride all the way back to Nebraska to tell Rafe her feelings, so you better not die. That's all I've got to say."

When she finished the job, she fell back against the cot and let her hands tremble all they wanted to. She had to get him out of those wet clothes and wrapped in a blanket, as well as build up a fire to keep him warm. There was enough wood in the box beside the fireplace to start up a blaze and in no time the shack was too warm. She fussed at herself for letting him get too hot, as she struggled with his wet boots and socks. When those were sitting in front of the heat, she unbuttoned his shirt and tugged at it until she was winded again. Finally, there was nothing left but his trousers. She reminded herself she already had the reputation of being a harlot, so she might as well have the game to go with the name. Still she blushed scarlet as high color filled her cheeks when she unbuttoned his trousers and pulled them down around his ankles.

Even if he died, she couldn't bring herself to take off his knee length undergarments. If pneumonia was going to set in, it would just have to do so. She wasn't brave enough to utterly take all his clothing off. Besides, she reasoned, his underwear would be dry in no time as hot as she had the room. Grabbing a blanket from the cot she wrapped it around him tightly, covering up all that soft fur on his chest, even though her hands itched to touch it. She cradled his head on the only pillow in the place, being careful not to let it touch the wound.

She needed a bandage but when he'd stocked the line shack he'd thought of everything but someone getting hurt.

A little food. Supplies to keep body and soul stuck together. Even a sewing kit in case their britches got ripped while working with the cattle. But no nice white bandages.

She remembered her petticoat and raised her heavy, wet skirt tail. White, thoroughly soaked and muddy. But the top part was still clean. By waving it in front of the fire, it would be dry in a few minutes. She jerked it off, took the ribbon out of the casing around the waist and using the small pocket knife she found in the sewing kit, shredded it into long, white strips. Sure enough, the thin white cotton dried quickly and she wrapped it around his head several times, then leaned back against the cot again.

She shivered in spite of the roaring heat in the small room. She'd have to shuck her own clothing or risk getting more than the sneezes. She peeled out of the muddy dress and the rest of her things until she had on no more than she did the day her mother brought her into the world. She went outside to wash the grime from her hair and the rest of her body in the coldest rain water she'd ever felt.

The rain cleansed her whole body as she rubbed the dirt away from her face, feet and hair. When she went back inside he still looked so pale and lifeless she wondered if his heart had quit beating. It was then that she saw the pump at the end of the cot, along with a big dish pan under it. She wrapped the last blanket around her body, tucked the ends under her arm and grabbed the pump handle. Sure enough rusty red water came spewing into the pan. By the time it was full, the water was only slightly nasty looking. She threw it out the door, being careful not to get her blanket wet.

Three pans later, it was running clear. She found a tin cup in the cabinet with the skillet and drank long and deep of the cool water. If Hoyt didn't come to soon, she'd have to force water down him. Willow had done that when Rafe was lying in the same condition in the back of the wagon.

She remembered well the first day on the wagon train. Five wagons didn't make it across the river before the ferries stopped running so Hank had left Rafe behind to bring them the next morning and catch up with the rest of the train. He was riding his horse across the river when a big snake spooked it, knocking Rafe out into the water. Willow shucked her clothes down to her undergarments and dived right in after him. She brought him up, pumped the river water from his lungs, sewed up the gash in his head, put on her overalls—much to the chagrin of her older sister— Velvet and led them to the rest of the train while Rafe recuperated in the back of the wagon.

Velvet remembered the way she'd cringed at her sister in men's clothing and suddenly wished she had a soft flannel shirt and a pair of overalls to put on. Hoyt groaned again but he didn't open his eyes. She laid her hand on his head but there was no fever. Not yet, anyway. She drew up enough water to wash her camisole and drawers. After she'd wrung them dry, she hung them over the back of a rickety chair she'd dragged up next to the fire. They should be dry in an hour she figured, by which time she'd have Hoyt's shirt and pants ready to dry next. Her dress could be last since she was finding the blanket worked very well if she kept it tucked tightly under her arm.

Willow had ended up marrying Rafe, but that didn't mean Velvet had even a slim chance of Hoyt returning her new found love. Even if she had stitched him up just like Willow had done to Rafe back at the first of summer. No, there were distinct differences in the situations, she told herself as she pumped more water to wash the mud from his shirt and trousers. Willow and Rafe hated each other when she sewed his wound shut; it wasn't until later that they fell in love. Today Velvet had figured out that she loved Hoyt Baxter, even with his hard heart and stubbornness, but there wasn't going to be a later for them. Hoyt didn't want her around him any more today than he did the first day he came home to find her dying in his bed. She'd just have to get over him. It wouldn't be easy but then love never was, she was finding out fast.

Hoyt twitched in his sleep. He was falling from a high cliff and there wasn't an end in sight. Just flailing arms and legs, trying to find something to hold on to. He felt the sizzle of a roaring fire and figured he'd missed the chance at Heaven. Now he'd never see Myra again, because he was sure that's where she and Weston both were.

He tried to open his eyes, to prove to himself it was just a dream, but they wouldn't cooperate. He heard the shuffling of bare feet on wood and wondered where he really was. His head throbbed and his back ached. Surely he wasn't dead. Dead meant no pain and he definitely hurt.

One eye finally opened barely a slit to peek past the lace edge of lady's under pants into a raging fire. It was still August, wasn't it? Why was there a fire going in the old shack? A clap of thunder roared outside and he shut his eyes against the pain that the noise brought. He was alive. He hurt like the very dickens. And he didn't give a hoot if he'd crawled up inside the shack on his own or if someone had dragged him. He was reasonably dry even though there was a storm raging outside. He shut his eyes and fog overtook him again.

Velvet wiped out the kettle with a rag and opened a jar of beans. She needed to make broth for him, not beans, but short of marching out there in the rain and shooting a steer for enough beef to boil for broth, she'd have to make do with what she had. By the time the beans had reached a boil, she'd managed to put together flour, a little leavening, salt and water for a pan of fry bread. She had to keep her own strength up, too, and she hadn't eaten since the jelly sandwich she had for lunch.

Hoyt smelled beans and heard the sizzle of bread. Was he really back in the cabin and not dreaming? His eyes fluttered open and there was Velvet bending over a fire, making fry bread. They were in the old line shack and a fierce storm was raging outside. Lord, but she was beautiful. He needed to tell her that and more, but his head hurt so badly. He reached up to find a bandage around his head. So he had hit something solid when he fell. Had she sewed him up then? He stared his fill of her, wrapped in a blanket, long dark hair flowing down her back as she shook the skillet and flipped the bread.

He'd found out right quick that he didn't want to die; and just as quick that he'd fallen in love with Velvet. He'd have to open up his heart and tell her, soon as he made a trip to the cemetery and explained it all to Myra.

"Oh, so you are awake," she turned to find him staring blankly at her. She wrapped the blanket tighter around her body, feeling a bit foolish at having nothing else on in his presence even if he was a full-fledged doctor. "You fell off your horse. It's back at the ranch. I found him in the barn and came looking for you. There's about fifteen stitches in the back of your head. Think you could sit up and get on the cot? It would be a lot more comfortable that that hard floor."

With her help, a lot of groaning, and nothing short of a miracle, the two of them managed to get him stretched out on the cot, without her loosing her precious hold on her blanket. His eyes wouldn't stay open but he had to tell her something. What was it? He drew his brows down in a deep frown.

"Do you think you could eat?" She asked.

"Not hungry," he muttered.

"Water?" She picked up the cup and held it for him to take a sip.

"Velvet?" He mumbled.

"Yes, Hoyt?" She touched his forehead. Still cool.

"When are you leaving?" He asked raspily, and then fell back asleep.

Chapter Thirteen

Hoyt's head throbbed when he opened his eyes. The storm had ceased and the moon filled the window in the line shack. Even though he had a tremendous headache, the agitation in his heart and soul had disappeared with the storm. He went back over the events and a grin played across his strong, handsome face. So it had taken a severe hit on the head to awaken him to the foolishness of the vow he'd made that day when he buried Myra and his son. Boyd always said that of the two of them, Hoyt had the hardest head and the softest heart. The smile on Hoyt's face just got wider and wider as he remembered Boyd and the good times they'd shared.

He had Velvet to thank for most of it. He would have awakened after a while, out there in the storm, but she'd taken care of him. Not only through the physical pain these past few hours but through a lot of mental anguish, too. *The dawning of the moon*, he thought, *is a symbol of my new serenity. I awake from turmoil and find a calmness inside that is wonderful.*

Velvet's breath was as soft as a butterfly's wings. He dropped his hand beside the bed and although he didn't actually touch her, the warmth of her breathing was as much a balm to him as the bandage around his head. He shut his eyes and slept peacefully for the first time in months.

The sun was high in the sky, doing its best to dry the wet earth when Velvet awoke the next morning. She was so stiff and sore from sleeping on the floor all night beside the cot that she feared she'd never get the aching muscles stretched out. Embers glowed in the fireplace but she didn't plan on making breakfast there. She was going to back that wagon up to the door, get Hoyt into it and they were going home.

He'd slept fitfully, murmuring in his sleep alternately to Myra and Boyd. She'd understood only a few words. Something about Boyd "liking her" and then a word or two about "loving you."

She sat up, wrapping the blanket securely around her bosom and then realized Hoyt wasn't on the cot. She frantically searched the small room and found him sitting in the ladder back chair, looking intently out the window. "You must be feeling much better," she said.

"My head hurts like I been kicked by a mule," he said.

"You able to ride to the house, or at least lay in the back of a mighty wet wagon?" She asked, ice dripping off every word. Of course his stupid head hurt. A full grown man didn't fall from a horse, flat out on a rock, knock himself out for hours and need stitches to close a gaping hole in his head, and it not hurt. Who did he think he was anyway? An angel straight from Heaven who didn't bleed? Quite frankly, she didn't care if he was an angel. He'd stated his position as clear as a church bell ringing on a cloudless Sunday morning the night before when he asked her when she was leaving.

Sure, you don't care, her conscience scolded. *If you didn't care about that man you wouldn't be hurting inside.*

You love him so admit it even if there's nothing you can do about it.

"Is that where breakfast is? I'm hungry," he said. Mercy, what had he said during the ordeal? Here, he'd just recognized his feelings for the woman and had the utmost intentions of declaring them as soon as he made one more trip to the cemetery to tell Myra and Boyd and she was as cold as clabber on a December afternoon.

"That's where breakfast is, Dr. Baxter. I see you've managed to put your pants on without help. Perhaps you could do the same with your shirt and then turn your back while I get dressed," she said. Whether Opal liked her or not was irrelevant right now: Velvet was going to the fort next week. She could stay a few days with Clara, and surely some kind of conveyance would come through the fort soon. Even a mail wagon would do. Staying in the house with Hoyt when they weren't even friends was one thing. To live there with him when she was in love with the man was quite another thing. Every day a piece of her heart would be ripped away to expose raw, aching nerves beneath it. She was a grown woman. She would do what she had to do to survive . . . again. A single tear fought its way to the brim of the dam behind her eyelids and slid down her face. She couldn't be in love with Hoyt Baxter. She just couldn't. It had been the circumstances, she tried to rationalize. The horrid storm; finding him hurt. That's what had given her the idea she loved the obstinate, overbearing martyr.

The floor rushed up to meet him and he had to grab the back of the chair when he attempted to stand. Velvet automatically reached for him, holding both arms around his waist until he regained his balance. All that dark hair covering his chest was soft, just as she'd imagined. His heart beat fast within his broad, muscular chest. She attributed it to too much exertion, not knowing that just the touch of her face against his chest produced the same effect on him as it did her.

She moved away from him as soon as she had steadied his equilibrium. "I'll get dressed now if you'll turn around," she said, gathering the drooping blanket back around her tightly.

"Yes, ma'am," he said, steadily making his way to the door. He opened it and looked outside. The cattle milled about, unhappy, but at least none of them had been hit by the violent lightning. One horse was still hitched to the wagon and it looked downright miserable but he'd take care of it when they got home. The sun had dried the wagon but he'd be willing to bet the seat wouldn't be totally dry. They'd have to take a blanket with them and sit on it or else have wet bottoms by the time they reached the cabin.

"My horse," he whispered, remembering it had fallen into a gopher hole.

"It came home with a sprained leg. I rubbed it down a bit but not nearly enough. You'll need to put liniment on it when we get back. I put him in the stall and threw some hay in," she said, buttoning her dress up to the neck. "I'll get these embers out and then we can go. Can you walk to the wagon or do I need to back it up to the porch?"

"I can walk," he said flatly. He'd fallen in love again and he'd thought that an impossibility. He'd had the most peaceful feeling in his heart—for a little while. Now the agitation, frustration and heaviness was back. Not for the same reasons, but it was there, eating on Hoyt until he wanted to go back to the fog surrounding him when he first opened his eyes and realized what had happened.

Sitting on the bouncing seat with the wagon, seeming to hit every single rough spot between the line shack and the cabin, Hoyt gritted his teeth and wished a hundred times he would have had the good sense to stretch out in the back of the wagon. But he'd be hung from that oak tree inside

Fort Laramie before he asked her to pull over and let him crawl into the back of the wagon. No sir, he'd bear up and when they got home, he'd go on about his work as if his head was in perfectly fine condition. She wouldn't ever know how his head felt like a stick of dynamite was exploding inside it, or that his heart was so weighted down he could scarcely breathe.

Velvet's thoughts went to her sisters. Which one was driving today? How far had they gotten by now and what was Willow doing these days? She'd have been married more than a month now, so she'd probably be settling down, running Rafe's ranch in fine style. She tried to constrain her thoughts but after a while they had a mind of their very own and nothing could make them remember anything; all they wanted to do was think of Hoyt. How the very touch of his arm brushing against her as they rode side by side on the small wagon seat made her flesh tingle. How, even with a bandage wrapped around his head, he was the most handsome man she'd ever seen. By the time they drove into the back yard, she was mad enough to chew up and digest weathered barn wood. He was twice as angry, and wishing he could go back to that numbness he'd known so long where he felt nothing.

"Well, hello," Clara yelled from the back door. "Where have you two been? We just got here and no one was home. There's soured beans on the stove, Velvet. Oh, my, what happened?"

"Hoyt was hurt out by the line shack yesterday," Velvet hopped down from the wagon after she set the brake.

"I can see that. Have you seen yourself, Dr. Baxter?" Clara giggled. "That bandage is lace trimmed. Kinda fancy for even a doctor. I betcha yesterday morning it was Velvet's petticoat."

"What's so funny?" Cyrus joined his wife on the porch. "Oh, my goodness, here let me help you Dr. Baxter. You are as white as driven snow. Let's get you inside and to bed."

"No," Hoyt said. "Not to bed. Just to the rocking chair. I'll be fine once I have some breakfast. The trail boss should be here today. Expected him yesterday. Guess the storm slowed them down, too," he explained as he leaned on Cyrus' big frame. "I can't be in bed. I have to deal with him for the cattle I have penned up."

"Well, these women can get some food ready. I'll go out to the barn and take care of the chores there. That cattle drive is about two miles south of the fort right now. Expect it will be here to your ranch in an hour or less. Maybe before they get here Clara could rebandage your head, though. That lace hanging down the back of your neck is a little funny. The trail boss might think he could take advantage of you lookin' like that, sir," Cyrus said.

"I'll rebandage it," Velvet said. "Cyrus, could you take these beans out to the hog lot on your way to the barn."

"Sure will," Cyrus picked the pot up and was out the back door, chuckling the whole way at Hoyt's bandage.

"I'll fire up the stove and make biscuits," Clara said. "I'd rather fix breakfast than mess with a head wound."

"Thank you, Clara," Velvet said. She drew up a pan of water and dropped a clean white washing cloth in it, along with a bar of pure lye soap.

"How'd you stitch it?" Hoyt asked, when she began to unwind the bandage. He now saw exactly what Clara and Cyrus found so funny. He must have been a sight in all that lace and ribbon bandage.

"With a needle and thread," she said shortly. "Be still. I've got to wash it and it's going to sting. I left the last stitch off so it could drain if there was an infection."

"Sterilize the needle?" He asked.

"Of course, and wound off the thread until I was sure it was clean. Poured pure whiskey in it to clean it out," she said, pulling up the thick hair and checking the wound. It looked dry and clean. No oozy mess at the end where the drainage hole was.

"I'm glad I wasn't awake," he said.

"Me, too. You would've screamed like a dying bull," she said.

"I would have not!" He declared emphatically. How dare she imply he couldn't take pain.

"Anyone would have, so shut up being Mr. Hero and let me clean this up," she rubbed the rag on the bar of soap and dabbed it to the wound.

"Ouch," he said with a jump.

"Point proven," she said.

"Enough arguing, children," Clara said, giggling from the table where she measured flour into a bowl for biscuits.

They both glared at her and she laughed even harder.

"Reckon you might need this," Cyrus said, bringing a pail of milk in the back door. "Cow seemed like she needed taken care of first. Horses and mules can wait a little while. She was hurting. Don't guess she'd been milked last night either?"

"No," Velvet shook her head.

"Just goes to prove, a woman don't think of the important things," Hoyt teased.

Velvet didn't think it was a bit funny. She'd saved his sorry life which was worth more than the cow's any day. "Hush. I could've milked the cow and twiddled my thumbs while you laid out there in that blinding storm and died. Cows can be replaced."

And he couldn't? Hoyt liked that idea.

"Here, I'll strain that," Velvet took the bucket from Cyrus. "Clara hasn't got any business lifting something that heavy."

"What about my head?" Hoyt carefully ran his fingers

over the wound. The stitches were close together and appeared to be doing their job well.

"Your head will be fine until I get this job done," Velvet told him bluntly. "It won't hurt it one bit to dry out a little. Matter of fact, if you were going to be inside all day, I wouldn't even rebandage it. It's not bleeding or oozing."

"Well, I'm not staying inside," Hoyt shuddered at the idea. "I'm going to the line shack with the trail boss to talk business about those cattle."

"Men!" Velvet mumbled, straining the fresh milk through a piece of thin white cotton material.

"I'll make gravy if you'll pour up some of that in a bowl," Clara offered. Something other than just an accident had gone on up there at that old line shack, she'd be willing to bet. Hoyt Baxter had a bit of a twinkle in his eye, not as much as he'd had when she first met him, but those big dark eyes weren't filled with sorrow anymore. She might just have to give Velvet a talking to if she wasn't smart enough to wake up and smell the roses.

"That sounds wonderful," Hoyt said. "Think I might have a cup of coffee while it's cooking?"

Velvet rolled her eyes. Now that they were among other people he was as cordial as a southern gentleman; not at all like that obnoxious fool who looked her right in the eyes last night and asked her when she was leaving. She grabbed a dish towel, picked up the coffee pot and tilted it forward over his favorite cup. When she handed it to him, her fingertips brushed his hand and she shivered.

"Coming down with a cold?" He asked.

"No, I am not coming down with a cold." Her voice, however, was filled with ice.

"Well, pardon me for asking," he snapped back.

They'd barely finished their biscuits and gravy when Cyrus opened the back door. "Hey, looks like I was wrong. They made good time or else they were closer to the fort than the scout thought, because here comes a couple of fellers on horse back that I'd swear are part of the cattle drive."

"Well, send them in," Hoyt said, glad that Velvet hadn't bandaged up his head.

Two men kicked the dust off their boots at the front door and were inside the cabin before Clara and Velvet could clear the table. "Hear you got some cattle you'd like to sell. I'm Clarence and this is Henry. We're on our way to Montana with a herd, hopin' to get there before the hard freeze. Could use a few more head to round out the sale."

"I'm glad to meet you," Hoyt stood, extending his hand. The room spun slightly but settled down fairly quickly. He didn't think it was a concussion in addition to the gash and unconsciousness. Most likely just the fact that he'd gone so long without food or water. "I'm Hoyt Baxter and this is Velvet, and our friends, Clara and Cyrus."

"Proud to make your acquaintances," Clarence said.

"Coffee?" Velvet asked.

"Why, that'd be nice, ma'am," Clarence pulled up a chair and Henry followed suit. "Man can talk business a lot better with a cup of coffee in his hands."

She and Clara busied themselves with a platter of sugar cookies and cups of coffee for the four men. Velvet thought they looked somewhat like tomcats. Friendly at a distance, but wary up close. Then she remembered why they were there. A business deal. Hoyt would want the best price for his cattle, and he probably didn't know a lot about it, being as how he was first a doctor. He'd lived in town his whole life until coming to Fort Laramie. Well, those two cattle men needn't think they were going to steal his cows right out from under his nose. No sir, not with Velvet in the kitchen.

"Why, ma'am, tea cakes to boot. You reckon you'd leave this man and run away with us. We'd pay you right well.

Old Cookie couldn't make up a batch of tea cakes if his life depended on it. If you cook for us, we'd take you all the way to Montana and cherish you like an angel the whole way," Clarence flirted.

If he'd shave that full red beard off he might not be a bad looking man, she thought, and it might be a way out of the house with Hoyt, who most definitely wanted her gone.

"Don't tease," she said, smiling.

Strings tightened around Hoyt's heart. If only she'd smile like that for him every day. Surely she didn't think this man was serious.

"Tease!" Clarence picked up his third cookie. "Not me. I'm serious as St. Peter on Judgment Day, darlin'."

"I've got a hundred and five head, penned up a mile north of here," Hoyt said, changing the subject abruptly.

"Well, then soon as me and Henry finish these cookies and try to talk your pretty wife into leaving your old sorry hide and going with us, we'll go look at them," Clarence said with a wink.

"I'm not—" Velvet started.

"She's not going to stay home," Clara butted in promptly. "She's going with you, Hoyt. You fellows can't see it, but he took quite a fall yesterday. Velvet sewed up the back of his head and she's going along with you all to look at the cattle. If you've got a spare minute when the sale is finished, come on back here and there'll be more cookies and coffee for you before you get on down the road."

"Yes, ma'am," Henry smiled.

"Now, me and Cyrus are going to get on back to the fort. We just drove out for a Saturday drive to get me out of the house," Clara said to Velvet. "Come and walk me to the buggy, Velvet."

"Why'd you do that?" Velvet said between clenched teeth when they were outside.

"Because, it's safer," Clara said. "Those men have been without a woman for a long time. All the way from Texas, probably. If they thought you was living there with Hoyt, they'd think the same thing Opal does and you might not be safe from them. You never know what kind of men they might be," Clara shook her finger at Velvet. "So you just go on letting them think you're his wife. It's only for today, Velvet. And guess what we found out at the fort. That's another reason I came out this morning. So you'd have a couple of days to get things together. There's a late wagon train on its way through. Going west. They'll not make it through the passes this winter, but they'll get close enough you could probably hire a stage coach to take you on down into California to your sister's house. It should be at the fort on Monday. That's day after tomorrow. I sure hate to see you go, but I'd feel bad if I didn't tell and at least give you a choice."

Velvet hugged Clara tightly. Two days and she'd be out of Hoyt's house. "Oh, Clara, I'm so excited I could shout. Just last night Hoyt asked me when I was leaving, so I know I'm a burr in his saddle."

"I don't think so, and don't be putting no stock in what a man says when he's in pain," Clara said. "Okay, Cyrus, I'm ready," she said.

Velvet waved until they were out of sight and then when out to hitch up the wagon again. She would have much rather stayed at the house and packed her things into the trunk, but Clara was right. If she didn't stay with Hoyt she might be in trouble. She grinned at that idea. She'd fought a war party with only her ingenuity, and had managed to live through the fever, but maybe she'd shouldn't continue to tempt fate.

Hoyt insisted on holding the reins as they drove back

out to the line shack. He, Clarence and Henry talked cows, Wyoming winters, and Texas summers the whole way. Velvet could have cared less about any of it. She was leaving and her heart was split down the middle. One half was glad and eager to get on with the trip, to see Gussie and the rest of her sisters. The other half was weeping uncontrollably for what could not be. Yesterday, she'd had the notion she'd confess to Hoyt that she'd just flat fallen in love with him, but today it wasn't even a possibility. He'd just kick that love back at her and she'd never get over the humiliation. No, it would be better if she shook his hand, thanked him for the room and board and left, without fuss or ado.

"Looks like a fine, grass-fed herd," Clarence said when they reached the pens. "Good stock here. Bring a fair price in Montana."

"It'll bring more than a fair price, and you know it," Velvet said with authority she didn't have. Lord have mercy, she'd never sold or bought a cow in her entire life. She'd been raised in the manse right beside the church in South Carolina and her grandfather didn't even have a milk cow. One of the congregation had seen to it a gallon of milk was brought to him every morning. Her grandmother wouldn't have known a bull from a heifer and didn't even know how to skim cream. Lizzy had taught Velvet that job along with dozens of others.

"I can take care of my own business." Hoyt raised an eyebrow and looked down at her. He might pretend she was his wife to save her reputation and possibly her virtue from these men, but she wasn't going to butt into his business, even if he didn't know a thing about fair prices.

"Of course, you can, darlin'," she said in a soft southern drawl. "But you are a bit addled from that fall."

Clarence laughed out loud. "We goin' to see a lover's spat?"

"No, sir, you are not," Velvet said. "What are you offering for these cows?"

"Dollar a head," he said without blinking.

"Then, it's been nice meeting you. We'll keep them before we sell that cheap. You know very well these cows will make your whole herd look a lot better at the final sale. They haven't been herded all the way from Texas and they'll hold that weight all the way to Montana," Velvet said, ignoring Hoyt's black looks.

"What'd you have in mind, Mrs. Baxter?" Henry rubbed his jaw.

"Twice that," she said, not knowing if the cows were even worth half that much.

"How about we split the difference?" Clarence said. "If you'll throw in the rest of the cookies you got baked up in there, we'll take them for that much. Give you gold in payment for a hundred cows."

"One hundred and five," Hoyt said. Velvet had just made a better deal than he could have hoped for yet he wanted to kick the fence post or hit Henry right between his beady little hazel eyes.

"Okay, a hundred and five," Clarence said. "And the cookies?"

"Of course," Velvet said. "You coming through this way or do you need to drive them back down to the rest of your herd?"

"My men will come right through here. I'll leave Henry here to take care of things and I'll go back with you two. Pay you up and bring my cookies on back. Henry, you say a word to the other trail hands about them cookies and I'll fire your sorry hide on the spot," Clarence said.

"Wouldn't dream of it boss," Henry grinned, showing off a mouth full of tobacco-stained teeth.

An hour later the deal was complete. Hoyt had a bag of gold that would make it possible for him to either go home to Louisiana or keep ranching the next year. Velvet disappeared up the stairs while he and Clarence shook hands. She opened her trunk and began to place her things back inside it. Less than forty eight hours and she'd be gone. She looked out the window in the loft, remembering the night she'd awakened from the fever induced stupor and saw the dawning of the moon. Well, she'd lived through the night experience and now it was full daylight without a cloud in the sky. Somehow in the darkness she'd fallen in love, but she couldn't just fall out of love now that the transportation she'd been waiting on was finally nearing.

She slammed her fist into the pillow and threw herself on the bed. She didn't want to leave, but she couldn't stay. Even if she told Hoyt how she felt, she'd be fighting a ghost the rest of her life. Myra was perfect. A tiny, beautiful doll who had his love forever. Velvet could fight a real person; she couldn't tackle a memory.

Hoyt shut the bedroom door and opened the armoire, fingering a pink robe Myra had loved. "I'll always love you," he said. "It's not that she's taking your place. There's room for both of you in my heart. But she won't ever know, Myra. Because I'm not going to tell her. She wants to be with her sisters, and she doesn't care a thing about me. I want a wife like you, who loves me."

He stretched out on the bed, careful to rest his head on the pillow in a way that it wouldn't touch the wound. His jaw ground back and forth in aggravation. Myra would have never gotten into his business like that. Even if it did mean much more money in his account, it still rankled him that Velvet had dealt with Clarence the way she did. He'd probably never see the man again in his life, but it was still a hard dose to swallow.

Velvet eased down the stairs and out the back door to go play with the kittens one more time. Tomorrow would be church in the morning; an at-home at Stella's in the afternoon and then finish her packing. She might not find another time to tell her five babies good-bye. She sat down in the hay and picked up two of them at once, burying her face in their softness and letting the tears flow freely. That Hoyt was angry with her was the understatement of the nineteenth century. He hadn't spoken a word to her on the trip back to the cabin, and now he was in that bedroom with the door shut tightly where he'd made a shrine to his dead wife. Hoyt sat in the rocking chair in his bedroom. Velvet snuggled the kittens. Pride separated them as surely as if it had been a raging river.

Chapter Fourteen

There was a soft nip in the morning air when Hoyt walked to the cemetery that Sunday. It would be a week or more before his horse's leg healed and it was just too much bother to hitch the other horse to the buggy just for a trip to the cemetery. Besides the walk would do him good. He could think about what he needed to say to Boyd and Myra.

As if all the talking would do a bit of good. Velvet sure didn't have the same feelings for him that he did her. She'd sulked all day yesterday. Spent half the morning out in the barn with that litter of kittens, and the rest of it up in the loft, coming down only to fix his dinner and supper. Her eyes were swollen and red, but there wasn't a reason for her to be crying. He hadn't even scolded her for taking it upon herself to butt into the male domain of business.

Now if that had been Myra, he thought. Then, as suddenly as a bolt of lightning streaking through the clouds, understanding dawned. It was so easy to make a perfect Myra. She wasn't there in the flesh to be anything but perfection. He could compare her to Velvet with those kind of standards and Velvet would always come up on the short end of the stick, as would any woman in the whole green, beautiful state of Wyoming. Myra hadn't been flawless when she was alive. She had a hot temper, too, so why had he created this spotless angel when she'd died?

He opened the cemetery gate and left it swinging rather than closing it. He sat down in front of the tombstones, trying to make sense of the emotional upheaval in his life. He'd made a solemn vow that he would honor Myra the rest of his life by never taking another wife.

And the vow has kept you from going stark raving mad, Boyd's voice seemed to float on the fall breeze toward him. *Do you think I'd want Clara to spend her whole young life decked out in black and mourning for a man who was so vain and prideful he wouldn't let you take off his leg?*

"Ah, but Boyd, you were never married to her? You didn't loose her because she was giving birth to your son," Hoyt whispered, hoping something of Boyd would continue to argue with him, but he didn't. What he'd heard from his brother was all he was going to get.

"Myra, I've fallen in love with another woman and I don't know what to do," he said. "She's not a thing like you. Every single feature is plain but put together they make a beautiful woman. Long, brown hair. The clearest blue eyes you've ever seen. A strange blue. Not like the sky, but more like a robin's egg. With a little green in them. Aqua is what comes to mind. She's not petite but she's not tall either. She's sassy and gets into my business but she knows her place in the house. When she smiles the whole world lights up with her beauty," he said.

Nothing happened. He didn't hear Myra's voice telling him to get on with his life. Nor did he hear her tell him that he'd made a promise and she was holding him to it. He bowed his head and prayed for the first time in months.

"Father," he whispered. "Give me a sign. Anything to help me understand what I'm supposed to do. Velvet can't love me as cantankerous as I've been, but I could be better. I could court her proper and show her that I wasn't always spiteful and mean. What am I supposed to do?"

"Do?" A voice said so close behind him that for a minute he thought God had actually descended from Heaven to have a visit with him. When he jerked around and found Rooster, a blush started at the back of his neck and set his ears on fire.

"Do about what? I just heard something about what are you supposed to do? What are you wanting an answer to, Hoyt Baxter?" Rooster asked.

Lord, he'd asked for a sign. Why did God send him Rooster Wilson? That wasn't a sign. It was a nightmare.

"Well?" Rooster asked.

"I don't think I can live up to the vow I made to never take another wife," Hoyt stood up, brushed the dried grass from the seat of his pants and waited.

"Well, that's good news. You got that woman who can cook so good still livin' with you?" Rooster asked.

"Velvet? Yes, she's still there," Hoyt said.

"Then sounds like to me you done got things worked out for you. Let's go on down there and sit on the porch 'til she gets Sunday dinner ready. Reckon she'd fry a chicken up if I picked the feathers for her?" Rooster followed Hoyt out of the cemetery.

"She went to church this mornin'. And she's lived in the cabin with me these past weeks but she's sure not interested in me. Not that I blame her. I've not been an easy man to live with," Hoyt said.

"Church! Good lord, man. You let her go to the fort after what I told you? Those women will roll her in tar and feathers and then hang her by the neck until Opal swears she's finally dead. What in the world were you thinkin', lettin' her go off like that?" Rooster yelled at Hoyt.

"I'll have to tell you about the cat fight. Don't you worry

none about Velvet. She held her own with Opal and I reckon if the devil himself showed up at church, she'd take care of that, too," Hoyt chuckled and repeated the story Cyrus told him about the incident.

"You goin' to fool around and let one of them soldiers over at the fort beat your time with that good woman," Rooster told him.

Hoyt didn't answer.

"Well?" Rooster's voice demanded a response.

"Well, nothing," Hoyt snapped. He'd asked for something to tell him he was doing the right thing, not a lecture from Rooster.

Don't look a gift horse in the mouth, Boyd's voice flitted through his mind.

"Always knew you was a proud man, Hoyt. Never figured you for a fool," Rooster said.

"Hey, wait a minute," Hoyt stopped midstride and glared at Rooster. "Don't you be calling me a fool. And besides, what are you doing back here, anyway? You said when you left that morning you wouldn't be back until spring."

"Changed my mind. Got to thinking about that woman's cooking and come to see if I might steal her from you for the winter. Figured since she was Jake's daughter, she could tell me stories, cook for me and maybe even learn to play a mean game of poker. I don't want a wife. But it might be almighty nice to have a little winterin' company. Give her my bed and I'll even sleep in the loft, I would," Rooster goaded Hoyt. He'd never meant to stay away from the fort all winter when he left. Indeed he had hoped that when he came back in a month he'd find the two of them already hitched. Looked like he was going to have to make Hoyt open his eyes and heart and see what was plain as the snout on a sow's face. The man had been in love with the woman weeks ago, and from that little prayer he'd overheard, Hoyt realized it now, too, and was too blamed stubborn to admit it.

"You can have her," Hoyt said, starting to walk again, faster this time.

"Good. Wouldn't want no hard feelins between us friends. Wouldn't even ask her if you was against the idea." Rooster had to bite his tongue to keep from laughing.

"No hard feelings," Hoyt mumbled. She wouldn't go off with Rooster. Or would she? The unanswered question seared his soul.

"Well, lookee here," Rooster stopped at the edge of the yard. "You didn't tell me we was havin' a party or I woulda took a bath."

Hoyt jerked his head up to see a dozen buggies parked near the barn. Children running and playing tag, some of them romping with Bummer, who looked like he had was in heaven; women setting up tables under the shade trees and covering them with all kinds of food; men lounging on his front porch as if they owned it. All he wanted was a few words to help him get through his dilemma. He certainly didn't ask God for Rooster and half the blasted fort to fall out of the sky on top of him.

"Hello, Dr. Baxter," Cyrus called from the porch. "We got a surprise party going on. Come and join up with us."

"Well, it sure is a surprise," Hoyt said.

"Yep, sure is. Women got it all together last night. Scout come to the fort yesterday morning before we come out here and found you all wrapped up in petticoats," Cyrus chuckled.

"There's a wagon train comin' through tomorrow afternoon," Cyrus continued. "Reckon it's the very thing Miss Velvet's been waiting for. She's already got her trunk loaded in my buggy and is plannin' to stay the night with Clara. Don't reckon there'll be much sleep goin' on. They'll visit all night, I'd guess. Anyway, the women folk up and decided they'd throw a surprise goin' away party for her. Of course, you and Rooster get to partake of the benefits."

Hoyd had prayed for help and his prayer had been answered after all. It had nothing to do with Rooster or the fort. He'd gotten it in the form of a wagon train. Velvet had already spent her last night in his cabin. There was nothing he could do now. The decision had already been made, most likely at the same time he asked God for help. "Looks like a good spread they're layin' out," he said.

"You know women folk. Give them a reason to cook and they're happy as larks," Richard said. "Hope you don't mind us intruding on your ranch. The kids are in heaven, getting away from the fort for a while. Women are chattering away like they've only got so much time to get all them words out of their insides."

"Don't mind at all," Hoyt said. Tomorrow he would go back to being a hermit. Rooster would stay the night in the barn and be gone by daybreak. His life would settle back into his familiar rut. *No it wouldn't!* He thought. He was fooling no one but himself if he thought it would, because a few weeks ago, a man by the name of Patty O'Leary had taken it upon himself to drop Velvet Jane Dulan in Hoyt's bed. Nothing would ever be the same again.

"Hello, Hoyt," Opal came around the end of the porch. "I come to tell you men to get your hands washed and get ready for the chaplain to say grace. Food is going to get cold if you don't get around. You, too, Hoyt."

Hoyt was stunned. Opal, at his place, after the way she'd talked to Velvet? Surely he was seeing things.

"Cat got your tongue or are you still acting crazy and not speaking to nobody from the fort? Well, that'll be hard today since there's so many of us here," Opal said in her coldest tone.

"Just can't believe my eyes," Hoyt finally said.

"Well, believe it. The general is here and he's hungry. I wouldn't be here but he set down his foot, and said I had to come or else I could go home to Virginia." She looped her arm through Hoyt's and led him toward the shade trees. "You know, I rather like that old man when he stiffens up his backbone. Makes me think of that young man I married a long time ago. Didn't run him around like a hoop back in those days. His word was the law. Yes, sir. In those days he was the boss and nobody crossed him."

Hoyt was absolutely speechless.

"Why don't you bury the hatchet and come on back to the fort where you belong? You are not a rancher, Hoyt Baxter. Oh, this ranch looks good, but it's a waste of your precious talents. We need a doctor. You need a wife and a job. Miss Dulan—I still think there's more gone on here than either of you'll ever admit—is leaving you, but Edith is still available. She always did look at you all sweet eyed."

Edith! Hoyt stifled a moan. Edith was a kind soul, bless her heart, but the general's youngest daughter grated on his nerves worse than any woman he'd ever met. Her buck teeth and high, whiny voice, along with that snort when she laughed, would have him straight jacket goofy in less than a day's time.

"What you ought to do is marry Velvet and make an honest woman of her," Opal continued, scarcely taking a breath. "You've done already ruined her reputation. If anyone on that wagon train figures out she lived her with you all this time, they'll spread the word. Trust me, Hoyt Baxter, a woman's reputation follows her just like her toilet water."

"Toilet water?" Hoyt asked, unable to make the connection.

"Oh, don't you play dumb with me, man. A woman's toilet water. The scent of it stays behind even after she leaves the room. That's the way with a woman's reputation. It's still there even when she's gone. Now here's the general. I hope I'm making him jealous," Opal said.

"I'm sure you are," Hoyt said graciously.

Velvet had barely parked Hoyt's buggy in the barn when she had seen the dust storm approaching from the fort. For several minutes she shaded her eyes with the back of her hand and watched them come. One after another parking in the barnyard, then a whole raft of people climbing out, including Opal, yelling, "Surprise." She could hardly believe her eyes, but then Clara hugged her tightly and told her they'd gotten together a Sunday afternoon picnic and all the women, along with their husbands and children from the fort, had come to wish her a good journey on the wagon train the next day.

She'd taken off her bonnet, wiped a tear from her eye and set about to help the ladies. Velvet met the children and told them to run and play all they wanted, even directed two little girls to the barn where the kittens were, and then looked up to see Opal coming across the yard with Hoyt in tow and the rest of the men, including Rooster Wilson, following behind them.

Miracles were alive and well in Fort Laramie, Wyoming, even if the one miracle she wanted so desperately couldn't be had. After the picnic, she'd leave Hoyt's ranch forever, and the problem with that was that her heart was right here in Wyoming. She'd be taking an empty shell onto California.

"Velvet," Hoyt said and nodded when Opal released him and went to stand beside her husband and daughter.

She nodded right back. "You asked me Friday night up there at the line shack when I was leaving. I can answer that now. I'm leaving tonight. Tomorrow, I'm going with the wagon train to Idaho where it will winter. The scout says that I can catch a stage coach from there on down to

California. It won't be too late for a coach to get through the passes but wagons go so slow they'd never make it. By Thanksgiving, I should be with my sisters again, Hoyt."

"I'm glad for you," he said.

"I'm sure you are more glad for you," she said. "You can go back to your own lifestyle without me interfering."

"I never said you were interfering," he protested.

"You didn't have to say it, Hoyt. It was written all over your face every day," Velvet said. "Now let's ask the chaplain to give thanks so we can feed these hungry children and men folks. Isn't it nice that the ladies have gone to all this trouble. And who would have ever believed Opal would come and bring the general and their daughter?"

Hoyt hoped his face wasn't giving away the way he felt right then. He sincerely hoped she couldn't see the desire to lead her right up to the chaplain and ask him to marry them rather than say a few words over all the food: beans, potato salad, a ham, a venison roast, a couple of fried rabbits, and a big bowl of corn on the cob, along with pies and cakes of every description.

"Join me?" Velvet asked him when she'd heaped her plate high with food. Not one bit of it looked good to her and she'd have trouble swallowing past the lump in her throat but she wouldn't hurt a single woman's feelings for anything in the world. Not even if it meant stuffing food that had no taste in her mouth.

"Be glad to," he said, loading his own plate and following her to a quilt where Clara and Cyrus were already eating.

"So when's the baby coming?" Hoyt asked Clara, making small talk to cover the pain in his chest.

"Tonight probably. This is the night the moon is its fullest. Granny Dempsy always said a baby would come when the moon was right. Something about the pull of the tides or some tomfoolery." Clara laughed. "Lots of things happen when the moon is right, don't you agree, Velvet?"

"Of course," Velvet said. "The dawning of the moon."

Hoyt raised his eyebrows and glanced in her direction, but she was busy tasting the potato salad. That had been his thought when he awoke from the fall on Friday night— that the dawning of the moon had brought about peace in his heart. How did she know that?

"Well, Cyrus, I think if you'll help me up, darlin', I'll make a run down to the little house at the end of the lot. And while you're up, would you check on Stella's boys? I don't see them anywhere. They can play in the hay loft but they shouldn't take their food up there, and I told Stella I'd help watch them while she takes care of serving tea and desserts," Clara said, not even trying to be imaginative in leaving Velvet and Hoyt together. They'd need a little time to get things straightened out if Cyrus was going to unload that trunk from their buggy before they left in the middle of the afternoon.

"So you're anxious to be gone?" Hoyt asked.

"Oh, my, yes. Can hardly wait until tomorrow. Gussie, Garnet and Gypsy, well, they'll be married by the time I get there, but to tell the truth I didn't want a husband any- way," she chattered nervously. "I was just along for the trip, you know. To get to know my sisters."

"You'd never heard of them before?" Hoyt asked.

"No, you remember the story Rooster told? None of us knew the other ones. Jake Dulan wanted a son but all he got was daughters. His wives kept dying of one thing or another, up until he married Willow's mother. After a year, he expected her to drop dead anytime, but she didn't and they figured out they just plain didn't like each other. So she went home to Mercersberg, Pennsylvania and he came on out west. Then Willow's momma died when she was a little girl and she ended up being raised by an aunt. None of us grew up with mothers or fathers. Just relatives."

"I see," Hoyt said. He'd have to grin and bear it, as the old cliché went. She didn't want to stay in Wyoming and who could blame her? She never did want a husband, but oh, but she was surely built for one. Those soft warm lips and eyes; that soft, southern voice and the way she could cook. Yes, she'd been groomed to be wife material. She just hadn't met the right man yet. When she came face to face with someone who made her heart melt like she did Hoyt's, why then she'd figure it all out.

He could just up and confess his feelings right then, but there was a possibility she'd feel honor bound to stay with him, thinking her reputation was ruined anyway. He wanted a wife who loved him so much she couldn't live without him. Not totally unlike Myra's love, yet maybe even a little deeper, because this wife would have to love him in spite of Myra being his first love.

Velvet didn't dare look up into those dark eyes. Not right then, or she would cry a milk bucket full of tears. She might even fall at his feet and beg him to let her stay with him, make an honest woman of her. He'd marry her, she was sure, if she pressured him. Those kisses they'd shared said he'd missed having a wife in his world, even if he didn't realize it yet. But Velvet didn't want a husband she had to coerce into marriage. No, she wanted one who loved her. Really, really loved her. Down deep in his heart. She wouldn't mind if he'd been married before and she could fully well accept that there would be times when he might even unwittingly compare her with the first wife. However, when he did, she intended that she'd be the one who'd come out in shining light because she was alive and the other one was a ghost in the past.

"Well, then, Velvet, I surely wish you the best," Hoyt said.

"And I you," she said.

"Thank you for all you've done for me," Hoyt said honestly.

"It was nothing. After all, I couldn't have done anything at all if you hadn't saved my life. I was sure I was dying when they put me in that wagon and Patty O'Leary offered to take me to the nearest doctor." She pushed her food around, hoping that would suffice as eating.

"You are quite welcome. You'll miss the winter in Wyoming. It's brutal. Sometimes we're snowed in for weeks and weeks. The only winter Myra and I had together here, I got called to the fort for a medical emergency, and left her here. Snow separated us for a solid week. I couldn't get back home and there was no way she could even get out of the cabin. We were so glad to see each other when I finally made it back." He laughed at the memory.

She shut her eyes and willed the tears not to flow. At least, he'd come far enough that he could remember his wife with a chuckle instead of one of those horrid black moods. Yes, she would miss Wyoming, whatever season it happened to be. She'd miss the blue skies, the snowy white clouds. She'd miss his dark eyes and the tingle in her body when their hands brushed at the supper table. She'd miss the kittens. She'd miss his kisses. She'd miss what couldn't be.

"We didn't get much snow in Carolina," she said, her voice only a little bit raspy. "I can't imagine having enough to build a snowman."

"Snowman. Sugar, we could build enough snowmen to make a fort full of soldiers about December or January," Hoyt said.

He'd called her sugar, just like southern gentlemen did to women they were flirting with. Inadvertently, but all the same, his tone had changed from those first days. Suddenly, she was mad at the wagon train. If he'd come around this far during the summer, then could it be possibly he'd continue to make progress until he was truly ready to bury the past and face the future? It was an interesting question but Velvet would be long gone before it was ever answered.

"What about you, Hoyt?" She asked finally, the silence becoming deafening between them.

"Oh, I don't know. I've had a few things on my mind as of late. I'll winter here, but who knows what the spring might bring?" He purposely evaded the question. If she was leaving, she had no right to know his business anymore.

"Hey, Dr. Baxter, you remember when you set my arm?" A young boy about ten years old ran up to their quilt, stopped abruptly at the edge and held out his arm.

"I sure do, Johnny," Hoyt said, glad for the reprieve. He and Velvet had said all that they had to say to each other. It was over, finished and done with.

"Well, I can throw a ball again, just like you told me I would be able to when I was a little kid and broke it." Johnny smiled, showing off the two big front teeth he'd have to grow into.

"I'm right glad," Hoyt said.

"You ever going to come back to the fort and be our doctor again?" Johnny asked.

"No, son, I'm not," Hoyt said. "But you know what, I see a big old chocolate cake over there and I bet me and you could talk Joy into cutting it if we sidle up next to her and tell her she's looking right pretty today."

"Ahh, I don't think I want chocolate cake that bad." Johnny blushed. "Besides she ain't as pretty as Miss Velvet, here."

"Well, thank you very much, Johnny." Velvet smiled and Hoyt's heart fell into a pulsating lump of jelly at her feet.

"Truth, it is," Johnny said with a high pitched giggle and ran off to play tag with his friends again.

"Indeed, it is," Hoyt held out his hand to help her.

"Well thank you, kind sir," she smiled right at him and braced herself for the shock. She was not disappointed. She made the mistake of looking right into his eyes when she was on her feet and for a brief moment she thought Opal was going to be able to deliver a scorching lecture to them both as their lips drew near to kissing. But at the last moment, the little girls she'd sent off to the barn came running helter skelter between them, begging for a kitten to take home with them.

"Of course, you may each have one," Hoyt said.

"Not the yellow one," Velvet said.

"Oh?" Hoyt raised an eyebrow.

"It's mine. Oh, I forgot. I'm leaving. But you could keep it here." She fumbled for words.

"Not the yellow one," Hoyt called after the little girls who raced back to the barn. "I took a liking to that one, too," he explained, holding her hand one more minute before letting it go. He'd keep that silly yellow kitten forever, and every time he rubbed its fur he would remember Velvet.

"In case we don't have time later, I want to say good-bye and thank you again," she said.

"We probably won't have time again," he said. "You'll have your duties with the ladies and I'll have mine with the men. So this is it, then. Good-bye, Velvet," he said, turning even as he said the words so she couldn't see the raw pain in his eyes.

In the middle of the afternoon, he stood on the porch and watched the buggies all leave his ranch in a line. Clara and Cyrus had waited until the very end, but Velvet didn't ask them to remove her trunk, so apparently she and Hoyt hadn't made any progress toward revealing their love to each other.

Hoyt waved until there was nothing but a cloud of dust. Before him, the woman he loved was leaving. Behind him, a house as empty as his heart awaited, filled with endless, long, cold days.

Velvet looked straight ahead, listening with half an ear to Clara rattling on and on about all the ladies at the picnic and how glad she was that Velvet was coming to have a night to visit before she left the next day.

Before Velvet was an adventure and a trip she no longer wanted. Behind her lay her heart. Living without it was going to be almighty difficult if not downright impossible.

Chapter Fifteen

Velvet tucked the quilt around her body and shut her eyes but she couldn't sleep. So much had happened in such a short time and thinking about it wanted precedence over a good night's rest. There was kindness and humor in Hoyt after all, and she wished him happiness, even though the idea of him kissing another woman the way he'd kissed her just about turned her pea green with jealousy.

The little room Cyrus and Clara had given her for the night was to be the baby's nursery when it got old enough to be out of Clara and Cyrus' bedroom. A narrow cot was against one wall. Colorful yellow feedsack curtains covered the windows and a rocking chair kept silent sentinel, awaiting the time when it would be put to use regularly. Cyrus had built two wooden boxes to slide under the cot and Clara had both of them filled with soft diapers and clothing for the new addition to their family.

Velvet wondered what it would be like to be a mother. To hold a newborn in her arms and know it was the product of an eternal love between two people. Thoughts of sitting in the rocker with a tiny baby cradled in her arms were playing in her mind when sleep finally erased everything and dreams took over.

"Velvet, wake up," Cyrus shook her arm gently. "It's time for the baby and I've got to go get Opal."

Velvet's eyes popped open and she sat up so fast that for a moment the room spun around her in circles. "Opal?" She asked.

"Yes, Opal is the midwife here at Fort Laramie," Cyrus said. "Could you go sit with her while I get my boots on and get Opal?"

"I surely can," Velvet was out of the bed and in Clara's room before she even realized she was wearing nothing but her night rail. She consoled herself in the midst of a fierce blush that it surely wasn't something Cyrus hadn't seen before.

"Oh, Velvet, I was just kidding when I said it would be tonight," Clara said. "Oh—" she moaned and grabbed the bed post above her head. "But the child isn't kidding about making an appearance tonight," she smiled when the pain had subsided.

"How close are the pains?" Velvet asked.

"Three minutes. I didn't want to wake Cyrus until I was sure. He's got to pull duty tomorrow night and needs his sleep tonight. But I guess he won't get much. Oh, here comes another one," Clara shut her eyes tightly.

"Don't do that," Velvet said. "Open your eyes, Clara. If you shut them all you'll see is the pain. Focus on something and it won't be so bad."

"Okay, I'll focus on your weird blue eyes until Cyrus gets back and then he's going to hold my hand and I'll look at him," Clara said.

"My eyes aren't weird," Velvet laughed.

"Yes, they are. They're not green and they're not blue and when you're mad at Hoyt they're so vibrant they almost glitter. Here comes another one," Clara said.

"That's barely two minutes apart," Velvet said.

"Well, that's the way it works," Clara told her. "Could you please get a cool rag and wipe this sweat from my face?"

"I sure will," Velvet said.

"Okay, okay," Opal came bustling in the door. "I'm here, Clara. Now let's see what's going on? Cyrus, you go put on some water to boil so I can clean the equipment," she ordered him with a point of the finger, and set down on the side of the bed.

Velvet returned with a wash cloth and washed Clara's face as Opal raised the sheet and proceeded to check the progress.

"So you're here?" Opal looked at her. "We left the picnic first. I wondered if you might unload that trunk and decide to stay with Hoyt?"

"No, ma'am," Velvet said.

Opal grunted, an idea forming even as she performed her duties as midwife. The baby was coming along fine. Shouldn't be more than an hour and it would be screaming and bawling. Clara was almost at the point when Opal would make her begin to push and with her wide hips, it shouldn't be any type of job at all.

"Oh, no," Opal shook her head slightly. "I think we've got a problem. I don't know if I can do this or not. Velvet you get on some clothes, girl, and go get Dr. Baxter. We need a real doctor to take care of this."

Clara turned white as the sheets covering her. "What is it Opal? Is my baby going to live?"

"We just need Dr. Baxter," Opal said. "Hurry up. Tell Cyrus to hitch up a buggy. Mine or his. Don't matter. I just want a real doctor in here. Go get him, Velvet."

Goose bumps the size of mountains played chase up and down Velvet's back as she hurriedly threw off her night rail and picked up the dress she'd laid out to wear the next day. She fastened the buttons as she ran across the floor and out the door. Cyrus handed her the reins and she was in the buggy before she realized that she was bare foot.

"Oh, well," she said aloud, snapping the whip over the horse's back to make him go faster. "It would have taken five minutes to button up those shoes."

Hoyt tucked his hands behind his head and listened to the night noises filtering through his window. After Velvet left with Clara and Cyrus he'd had a house cleaning in his bedroom, taking all of Myra's things from the armoire and packing them into the trunk she'd brought with her from Louisiana. He'd hauled it up to the loft and set it beside the cradle. Uncovering the cradle, he ran his hands over the fine wood and stopped to touch the soft things Myra had sewn while they waited for Weston to be born. He picked up the black cloth and started to cover both the trunk and cradle when a soft breeze blew through the open window.

For just a moment he stood very still, expecting to hear her voice. But there was nothing but the breeze, and with it a deep inner peace in his soul. Myra had said good-bye with her last breath. She'd told him she loved him. Now it was time for Hoyt to say good-bye and he didn't need to cover the past with a black cloth to do it. He folded the material gently and laid it over the baby clothes.

He was thinking about giving them to Clara for her new baby when he fell asleep. He dreamed of Myra and she fussed at him for taking so long to tell her good-bye, saying that she had things to do and couldn't wait around forever for him to get on with his life. Then suddenly the front door slung open, as did his eyes, and someone was running across the floor into his bedroom. He was attempting to prop himself up on one elbow when Velvet grabbed him by the shoulders and began to shake him.

"Hurry up, Hoyt. Clara is having the baby and there's trouble and Opal said for me to come and get you and I forgot to put on my shoes and my feet are cold and you've got to get dressed I'll get your bag while you get your boots we can go in Cyrus' buggy," Velvet said, her voice in a panic.

"I'm not going to the fort. I'm not a doctor," Hoyt said, taking her hands from his shoulders. "Now settle down. Opal is a fine midwife. She's delivered more babies than I have, if the truth be known."

"You are going to the fort," Velvet said between clenched teeth. "I don't know a blessed thing about Opal's abilities. But she said she needed you to be there and you're getting out of that bed and you're going to the fort. Do you understand me?"

"I understand you just fine, Velvet Jane Dulan. I also know what I'm not doing," Hoyt said. Mercy, but she was a handful when she was angry.

"Oh, yes you are!" Velvet ran back into the living room, picked his shot gun off the wall above the mantle, quickly shoved shells in both chambers and pointed it right at his chest. "Now get up and get your clothes on, Dr. Baxter. You are going to the fort."

"Shoot me," he taunted, pushing the covers back to his waist and sitting up in bed. "If I'm dead then she sure won't have any help, will she?"

Velvet lowered the gun to the bump under the sheets where she supposed his knee was. "I reckon you could still deliver a baby with a busted knee, then you can die. I don't care if you are dead but Clara is not going to loose this baby because you're too blasted stubborn to set foot on the fort."

"Is it that important to you, Velvet?" He asked.

"It is," she said. "Clara is the only one who stood up for me in that place. If it hadn't been for her, the rest of them would've never come around. I won't let her or that baby die even if it means I go to jail for shooting you. I figure I can drag you there even with a busted up leg."

"Okay, okay, put that blunderbuss away." He threw his legs over the side of the bed and picked up his trousers from the back of a chair. "What exactly did Opal say was the problem? Breach? Feet first? Too big? Where is my bag?"

"She didn't. She just said for me to waste no time bringing you back. Your bag is sitting beside the door collecting dust, I'm sure. It's most likely where you put it the last time you used it," she said, hanging the gun back on the rack and hoping he didn't renege on his word.

"Well, okay, Velvet, you've won the fight. Now let's go take care of this birthing. I'm warning you though. The last baby I delivered was Weston and I lost both baby and mother. I told you before, I've lost my touch," he said.

"You saved my life so evidently you've got it back," she said bluntly and hopped up on the buggy seat. "You can drive back. My hands are shaking so bad, I don't think I could hold the reins."

He snapped the whip and the horse took off at a gallop. Velvet's long braid whipped around her face and slapped against this shoulder. Without dropping the reins, he carefully handed it back to her, loving the sparks flying between them when their fingertips touched. So it took a determined woman, a new baby having trouble coming into the world, and Opal to bring him back inside the gates of the fort, he thought as he stopped long enough to tell the sentinel who he was and what his business entailed.

He had his bag in his hand and was already in the small house by the time Velvet could catch her breath from his driving ability and the exhilarating speed. She dashed through the front door just in time to hear the first pitiful wailing of a new born and Hoyt Baxter literally blow his top.

"Opal, I ought to string you up by your toes, you old witch," he shouted. "This is no emergency. That baby is so tiny, Clara could have had it without any help at all."

"Shut your mouth, Hoyt," Opal said. "And take this child. I've got another one coming right behind it."

"Twins?" Hoyt whispered.

"Good grief, man, talk in a normal voice. First you are yelling so loud you'll wake the dead then talkin' so low I can't even hear you. I'll take care of this one. You come on down here and deliver this next one," Opal said. "Figure you got about five minutes so get scrubbed up. The water is hot and the soap is free."

"I'm going home," Hoyt said.

"Sure you are, right after you deliver this baby," Opal said.

"You can do it, Opal," he said.

"Probably, but I ain't going to. Be good for you to bring a live one into the world. Take away the pain of the last time when things didn't go right. Wasn't your fault. Never was. The general sure enough made that clear enough to me when you turned Velvet Dulan loose on this fort. Now scrub up or catch it with dirty hands. I think Clara's about tired of waiting for you," Opal said.

Hoyt scrubbed up.

The second baby boy was just slightly bigger than the first one, but Clara had no trouble bringing him into the world. Both little boys appeared healthy with good lungs even if they were small. Hoyt tied the cord off in two places and deftly cut between them. Then he handed the child to Clara, who cooed and kissed on the wrinkled, red baby until it was time to give him to Opal for his first cleaning.

"Two of them," Cyrus said from the doorway. "Got a head start on the world, don't we Clara?"

She held out her arms and he crossed the room to hug her gently. Velvet stood in awe of the whole process. Opal, cleaning first one baby and then the other; Hoyt, performing the rest of his duties as a doctor. Two sweet little boys for Clara and Cyrus to raise together. Suddenly tears filled her eyes, flooded down her cheeks and dripped onto her dress. She wanted to be around when those little fellows took their first steps. She wanted to cuddle them and help Clara rock them.

But she was leaving in a few hours.

Opal wrapped the second one in a soft blanket and handed it to Clara who was already busy nursing number one. "I'd think you got your job cut out for you, but I bet Hoyt here could tell you even better than I could, seein' as how he and Boyd were twins. I bet he could tell you stories that could make your hair turn plumb white overnight."

Hoyt just smiled. "Opal, help me change this bedding and then I think we can all go home and get a good night's rest."

Velvet wiped the tears away with the back of her hand and disappeared out into the darkness. Clara didn't need a maudlin friend at this time. She needed smiles and happiness surrounding her, and as soon as Velvet got control of herself, that's exactly what Clara would have.

"So, I'd say you got something else to take care of before you go home to a good night's rest," Opal told Hoyt as they expertly worked together to change the sheets without disturbing the baby's first meals.

"Oh, and what would that be? You got another woman in an emergency situation here?" Hoyt asked.

"Yes, I do," Opal said.

Hoyt cocked his head to one side and eyed her from under heavy dark lashes. "Who would that be, pray tell?"

"She's standing out there on the front porch, trying to get control of her tears right now. She's in love with you but she's a lady. Sure enough galls me to have to admit it since I'm never wrong about people. But I was this time, Hoyt Baxter. That Velvet Dulan is a real lady and I was dead wrong about her. But I'm not wrong about the fact that she's in love with you and a lady don't propose to a man. It's the other way around. So I'd say it's an emergency situation we got here. You only got a few hours to take care of it. And one other thing. Your enlistment is up. That's a fact. But starting tomorrow morning, you've got a job to do on this fort. The general will pay you as a civilian doctor. That is if you don't go out there and take care of the emergency. If you do, the general will give you a week to honeymoon with Velvet and you can show up for work the following Monday. Guess it's your choice now," she said.

"She's right," Clara said. "Velvet loves you."

"Yes, she does," Cyrus said, nodding.

Hoyt picked up his bag and walked out the door. They were all crazy. Opal, more than any of them. Demanding he come back to the fort to work as a doctor. Tonight was a special instance. He could have either come with Velvet or she would have taken his knee cap off with that shotgun, dragged him out to the buggy by his hair and brought him to the birthing, leaving a blood trail from the ranch to the fort. But they were wrong about her loving him. She'd told him quite honestly that she couldn't wait to be back with her sisters.

"Violet?" He said when he reached the porch and walked past her to toss his bag on the buggy seat. "Tell Cyrus I'll return his buggy tomorrow."

"I will," she said past the lump in her throat.

He flicked the reins and the horse took two steps forward. Velvet stomped her foot so loudly he turned back to see if she'd fallen off the porch.

"What happened?" He drew up on the reins and found her standing beside the buggy in three easy strides.

"What happened?" She repeated the question, her blue eyes glowing by the light of the moon. "What happened is that you are the most cantankerous male I've ever known. You beat my grandfather to pieces when it comes to stubbornness and he was a professional at it. You are hateful, spiteful, and you are living in the past. So I don't know why I even like you, must less love you, but I do. And that's what happened, Hoyt. I fell in love with a man who could never love me. I'm not little and cute. I'm just plain old Jane, like you said yourself when I first got dumped on your bed. But that's the way I feel, and I just thought you might ought to know before I leave tomorrow morning."

Had he heard right? Had she actually said she loved him?

One minute he was sitting in the buggy; the next he was on the ground with Velvet in his arms, her head tilted back and kissing her. "Oh Velvet," he said when he came up for air, but didn't let her out of his embrace, "I love you so much. I just thought I didn't have a chance. I've been married. I made mistakes. I don't deserve you. And don't you ever say you are plain Jane again. You are Velvet, the most beautiful woman in the world to me."

She wrapped her arms tightly around his neck again and brought his mouth down to hers for another searing kiss.

"Ouch," he said. "Remember I've got stitches back there," he grinned, his whole face beaming when he pulled back from her kisses.

"I'm sorry," she laughed. A real, heartfelt laugh just for him. "I'll have to be gentle with you the rest of the night, won't I?"

"Well, let's go wake up the chaplain," Opal said from the front door of Clara's small house. "You ain't goin' back out there to that cabin after all those declarations and expect me to believe nothing will happen. I mighta been mistaken the first time but I won't be this time."

"Hoyt?" Velvet drew back and looked into his face.

"Would you marry me?" He asked simply.

"Yes, sir, I surely will," she said.

An hour later they were on their way back to the cabin, her trunk reloaded in the back of Cyrus' buggy. Hoyt kept one arm firmly around her and drove with the other one. Velvet's whole body, heart and soul hummed with contentment.

"I've been thinking about going back to Louisiana before this war breaks out," he said after a while. "What would you think of that, my love."

She smiled, liking the way he'd said she was his love. "Let me tell you a story. When Willow arrived at St. Jo, Missouri, the stage coach stopped at the Patee House and she was expecting a ramshackle hotel, not a big sprawling thing that had more than a hundred rooms. Anyway, she was standing there, in awe of the building and the stage driver said that at that time of year the whole hotel was full of people getting ready to go to the promised land. He called them fools because there wasn't no such thing as the promised land."

Hoyt wondered where she was going with this story but he kept quiet and let her talk as he drove the buggy into the double doors of the barn. He helped her out, held her close to his chest, still astonished at the way things had changed in the course of only a few hours.

"Well, the way I figure it is that he was wrong, Hoyt," she said watching him hurry through the basic job of putting Cyrus' horse in a stable and tossing him a fork full of hay.

He turned around and picked her up, carried her across the yard, kicked the door open with the toe of his boot and then back shut with his boot heel, and crossed the living room. He laid her gently on the bed, and kissed her again deeply, savoring the faint smell of roses, tasting luscious lips and nuzzling her neck.

"Yes, he was wrong," she whispered, her warm breath tingling against his ear. "You see as long I'm with you, I don't care if we're in Wyoming, on a ranch, or living in the middle of Fort Laramie, or even in a house right in the middle of a town in Louisiana. Anywhere I am with you, it's the promised land. Now kiss me again—please."

He gave a quick thanks to God for hearing his prayer and sending him Velvet. Then he bowed his head and kissed her, joining two souls forever in their own promised land.